THE
CONVERTIBLE
LIFE

a novel

SEAN MEYRICK HANLEY

Red Baron Press
New York

RED
BARON
PRESS

ISBN: 0615750257
ISBN-13: 978-0615750255

POUR MA RAISON D'ÊTRE,

MARIO BRASSARD

ACKNOWLEDGMENTS

I WOULD LIKE TO THANK THE
FOLLOWING PEOPLE FOR THEIR
LOVE, INSPIRATION, SUPPORT &
EYE-STRAIN DURING THE
ENDLESS RE-WRITES

LAURIE GRAFF
TODD GRAFF
GEORGE & ANNE HANLEY
CHAD HAYDUK
MATTHEW WILLIAM HUNTER
JOY PARISI
RAFAEL PAZ
JACK ROBBINS
GABRIEL SCHAEL
ALEXANDRA SHELLEY

AND AN EXTRA SPECIAL THANKS
TO MY BEST READER,
BEST LISTENER,
BEST ADVISOR,
& VERY BEST FRIEND IN THE WORLD,
WITHOUT WHOM THIS NOVEL
WOULD NEVER EXIST

DIANE DAVIS PETERSON

9

"EVERYBODY HATED ME. The cast and crew. The hack director who had taken twelve hours to film a thirty minute sitcom. The writers and producers. The network suits. The studio audience who had mutinied and abandoned ship. My homophobic, latent homosexual stand-in who snuck peeks at me during wardrobe fittings. The paid laughers who were hired to sweeten the laugh track even though they had soured hours ago. Danny Pintauro who played the lady boy on *Who's The Boss?* [1] My overrated agent. My over-paid publicist. My overweight personal trainer. My boyfriend, Adam Roth. My executive producer, Adam Roth. The basket-case we referred to as Mommie Dearest.[2] Our dead father. Even you. My goddamn twin brother. *Especially you.*

EVERYBODY WAS HATING ME because everybody hated you, but as usual I'm getting ahead of myself. It was about T minus two hours before the taping when you appeared out of nowhere and burst into my trailer while I was memorizing last minute script

---

[1] Danny Pintauro was the effeminate child-actor on *Who's the Boss?* who (spoiler alert) came out as gay in an interview with the National Enquirer tabloid in 1997.

[2] *Mommie Dearest* is a 1981 biographical drama film portraying Faye Dunaway as Joan Crawford, a driven actress and compulsively clean housekeeper who tries to control the lives of those around her as tightly as she controls herself. If the term, "No wire hangers!" means nothing to you, then perhaps you should put this book down now and sign up for a Netflix membership.

changes. 'Thom!' you screamed nonchalantly, like you hadn't ignored my calls for months, like you didn't need something. You looked like shit, but I had expected you to look worse. I was shocked they let you onto the studio lot until I realized that the guards assumed you were me. That you let them assume you were me. That you were pretending to be me. *Again.*

I was freaking out over new dialog, this one hellish line in particular since I hadn't slept in days and my brain had stopped remembering. I was relieved when you uncharacteristically offered to pick me up a Chinese chicken salad from Chin Chin[3] because it would give me more time to run my lines. Unfortunately I gave you money.

Cut to an hour and a half later when you returned to my trailer, most likely from doing lines with your dealer, possibly from shooting some low-end internet porn, probably both. You were clench-jawed and salad-less. Your shaky hand flicked the noisy flint roller of your mini-Bic while your eyes darted around the room with neither rhyme nor reason. You barely shrugged when I asked where you'd been. You began closing all the shades before handing me a pile of urgent, day old messages that my assistant gave you because she also assumed you were me.

The messages were from my New York agent at Innovative who I'd been blowing off since I was contemplating switching my representation to Creative Artists Agency. In anticipation of *Wall Street Widows* receiving a full-season pick-up, C.A.A. had been doing everything shy of rimming me in order to ensure my defection. Yet Innovative had already negotiated a deluxe, oversized trailer into my contract—with substantial pop-

---

[3] A popular Los Angeles chain of "healthy", Gringo-style Chinese restaurants where an actual Chinese person would not be caught dead working, or eating for that matter.

outs. *On both sides.* But, as you eagerly pointed out, 'Yours isn't nearly as big as Neil Patrick Harris's.'

'Who, incidentally, is repped by C.A.A.'

You flicked your mini-Bic at me with disdain, 'Really, Thompson?' Besides Mommie Dearest you were the only one used my full name. Probably because you knew it bothered me.

I had to worry about each and every word I said as anything could set you off, 'I was just saying.'

'Of course you were. You're always just saying. Unless of course you don't have any names to drop. If that's the case then what's the point at saying anything at all?'

Jealousy oozed from your lips as you peeked through the window shade and peered into the evening sky as your eyes darted around looking for God knows what. It was obvious you were trying to pick a fight so I pulled out the latest script changes and started going over my new lines.

'Could you please not do that?'

'Do what?'

'Talk out loud.'

I held up my script that was collated with pages more diverse and colorful than a box of crayons, 'Do you see these changes? While you were busy not buying me a salad the P.A. delivered a whole new set of goldenrod pages that I need to learn before the audience arrives. Goldenrod! Until tonight's show we've never gone beyond salmon revisions. Or maybe buff.'[4] You ignored my outburst and kept peering through curtains on all sides of the trailer, at all angles, as if you were looking for a sniper. 'What are you doing?'

---

[4] Revision pages for television shows are distributed on colored paper, a different color for each set of revisions. The progression of colors varies from one production to the next, but a typical sequence would be: white, blue, pink, yellow, green, goldenrod, buff, salmon, cherry, tan, ivory, white (this time known as "double white"), and back to blue ("double blue").

You flicked your mini-Bic nervously, methodically, and then said, 'You haven't noticed the helicopters?'

'No,' I answered hesitantly in the form of a question, praying you wouldn't elaborate.

'I'm sorry I couldn't be a good little slave and get your dinner but they've been following me ever since I left the soundstage.'

'Who?' I asked with immediate regret.

'I don't know. Obviously some government agency. The FBI? The CIA? The DMV? I had to hide in the underground parking garage so they couldn't trace the signal from my cell.'

The most upsetting part about your story was that you whole-heartedly believed it. I had long ago learned from my teenaged disputes with Mommie Dearest that it was fruitless to quarrel with a drug addict who valued arguing over the argument itself. Since it was obvious you were tweaking I thought it best to be supportive, 'Why didn't you just turn it off?'

That's when you completely lost your shit and went on some tangential tirade accusing me of stealing your ninety-nine cent lighter. You screamed and kicked the walls of the trailer until my Assistant knocked on the door to make sure everything was okay. You kept screaming for a good ten minutes after I sent her away until I finally pointed out, politely, 'Are you talking about the lighter in your hand?'

I HADN'T SEEN YOU so enraged since that summer between sixth and seventh grade when we got shitfaced after raiding Mommie Dearest's liquor cabinet. It wasn't long before we were rummaging through her pharmaceuticals for her valium stash which she routinely hid after catching on to the fact that we were replacing them with aspirin that you dyed expertly with blue food coloring. Anyway.

The ancient prescription was hidden deep in the recesses of her overflowing medicine cabinet. It was just a generic penicillin from Kerr's Pharmacy that we had no use for, but it was the person's name on the bottle that sent you into a tizzy. You grilled me as if I was withholding information on who exactly Jackson Zapf was and why his medication would be hidden amongst Mommie Dearest's vast assortment of colorful prescriptions.

'How am I supposed to know who he is? We were only two years old when it was prescribed!'

'That bitch was cheating on Daddy!'

'How do you jump from antibiotics to affairs?'

'Now we know her motive for killing Daddy!' And with that you plucked Jackson Zapf's prescription from my frozen hand and went downstairs to confront Mommie Dearest in the living room.

I hid behind the door of her daintily floral-wallpapered sewing room while you shrieked at her, 'You're nothing but a dirty, filthy, lying whore! How could you do this to our father? How could you lie to us?' Typically an expert debater, it was eerie the way Mother never responded to your tirade. She didn't defend or even explain herself. She didn't even bother to deny your accusations. Midway through the argument you raced out of the house and grabbed the keys to Daddy's Porsche during some drunken attempt to escape our suburban prison.

I watched from the upstairs window as you opened the door to the detached garage. I didn't believe you could leave me with her, let alone that you would. But you did. Or at least you tried. Even back then you didn't think twice about abandoning me. Forget about the fact that you were twelve and had no idea how to drive a car, let alone a stick shift that had been chained to a chestnut tree. You rarely thought things through, even back then.

I raced outside as the car's gears ground like fingers down a chalkboard. The reverse lights briefly lit up the dark garage before the Porsche shot out of its eight year hibernation like premature ejaculate. It was like a rocket, spitting stones from the white pebbled driveway deep into orbit until you reached the end of your leash. The car jerked and eventually stalled in the dying hedge, but not before the chain ripped off the convertible roof. You were crying, completely defeated, caressing the childhood scar on your forehead from The Accident which had partially opened up when your face hit the steering wheel. Mommie Dearest claimed that scar was the only way she could tell us apart.

Your whimpering was muffled by Moya's pantyhose angrily scraping together beneath her black and white uniform as she ran outside to collect you from the wreckage. She wiped the blood from your forehead with her apron, 'What the devil got into you?' In lieu of answering through your hyperventilation, you just handed over Jackson Zapf's prescription and accepted Moya's hug as collateral.

Although the Porsche was barely damaged, it was never driven again. In lieu of having it repaired, Mommie Dearest shackled it to the chestnut tree with a steel linked chain she had delivered from the True Value. Unlike Daddy's car, Mommie Dearest had you towed away for repair the very next day. It was months before you returned, having been kicked out of the first of a string of boarding schools to which Mommie Dearest had banished you.

At the time we thought it would have been impossible for her to sever our relationship. Identical twins were far too connected for something like that to happen. We were practically the same person and would forever be connected in a way that neither time, distance, nor boarding school could overcome. And we were right. Mommie Dearest was definitely not the one who put the wedge between us.

IT WAS LESS than thirty minutes before the studio audience was due to arrive, yet you continued to scream at me while I was trying to memorize those grueling last minute script changes. You paced back and forth like a rabid dog, cornered in the 182 square feet of my expansive trailer as your deep-seated resentment began to foam from your mouth.

'When was it exactly when you turned into such a selfish, demanding Hollywood fuck-wad who doesn't give a shit about anything but himself?

I was speechless, mostly because there was no point in answering your rhetorical question. Unfortunately my silence did nothing but enrage you further.

'What? You have no answer? But we're talking about your favorite subject: *you!*' You barely took a breath into your oxygen-starved lungs before you continued to berate me, 'If you think for one second that your success has anything to do with talent, then you are drowning in total fucking denial.' Unfortunately it was the only thing you'd said since you'd arrived that made the least bit of sense.

I was afraid to respond, let alone defend myself as you segued into your favorite tangent, 'You are nothing but a human parasite! How does it feel to be living my life after you hijacked my career?' Self-pity fueled your fury like gasoline, 'I was, supposed to be the one with the ridiculously rich boyfriend with the ridiculously cheap toupee! The one living in the Beverly Hills, Spanish-style McMansion whose landscaped lawns were tended to on

Mondays and Thursdays by a middle-aged Mexican named Nacho! I was supposed to be the one starring in this shitty sitcom!'

You stared at me for a long beat while I attempted to process the extent of your brooding self-victimization in your entitled Veruca Salt[5] campaign. Then I responded, 'I want an everlasting gobstopper and I want one now, Daddy!'

I wasn't sure if you were upset because I was making fun of you, or possibly because my Willy Wonka reference had somehow desecrated the memory of Daddy? Regardless, you stormed out like an unpredictable tornado and slammed my trailer door so hard that it shook me almost as much as you had.

When we were younger I used to pray that I had done something so exceptionally horrible, so incredibly tragic, so emotionally traumatizing that you were never able to recover—let alone forgive me. If that was the case then your constant abuse might have been justified. I'd spent years trying to recollect the seminal moment which bore your deep-seated grudge for me, but that elusive, reprehensible experience, which was apparently utterly unforgettable to you, was equally unmemorable for me.

SMASH CUT TO the middle of the taping on the soundstage. The set was especially cold that day. Night? Morning? Who knew what time it was outside of that windowless, soundproofed building. Inside it was always as brain-freezing cold as a frozen margarita gulped too quickly. However that particular day seemed so unusually cold that it reminded me of a recent, teeth-chattering *Late*

---

[5] The other obnoxious little girl who doesn't turn into a blueberry in the 1971 version of *Willy Wonka and the Chocolate Factory.*

Show appearance where I was expected to promote the new show or possibly talk about my stint on reality television when I was voted off the first season of *Big Brother*.[6] But none of that really matters since Letterman ended up bumping me with no explanation. At all.

I expected to see my breath steam its way through the artificial morning flood lights that poured through the fake Tribeca loft's missing windows. The panes had been removed so they wouldn't produce reflections of gaffers, lights or cameramen, but you surely know about these filming tricks from all your misadventures in gay porn.

We should have wrapped hours ago, long before midnight, yet there we were in the middle of the seventh or possibly eleventh take of the last scene. A relatively simple scene, but for the life of me I couldn't spit out this one insipid, tongue-taunting line of dialog. Which now, of course, I can't seem to forget.

The Assistant Director announced, as if to scold me into submission, 'Here we go people! In Three... Two...' but then, instead of saying 'One,' the A.D. simply held up his index finger, as if he was preoccupied with an important phone call and needed a minute. I, of course, needed several.

BUTTERFLIES DON'T BEGIN to describe the feeling I had every time a new goddamn scene was about to be shot. My chest would pound as if it was full of dragonflies while I'd wait for my heart to go into a free fall during that brief, yet ridiculously endless moment before the red light atop Camera Three illuminated my

---

[6] A televised reality game show, the first season of the worldwide sensation *Big Brother* was hosted by Julie Chen, a.k.a. The Chenbot, and was wildly unpopular in the U.S.

peripheral vision. During an earlier scene I'd convinced myself that I was having a heart attack. I made the Phone Page call the Universal Studios' medic, who, though thoroughly annoyed, diagnosed me with having yet another panic attack. The feeling of everybody patiently waiting for me to fuck up was nauseating. The only thing about acting I found the least bit gratifying was the paycheck.

Take twelve. Possibly thirteen. And yet my dialog continued to elude me. The Director gave me a humiliating line reading over the PA system. Even he had the words memorized. *'If something unpleasant happens on Wall Street and there are no inside traders around to initiate a sell-off, did it really happen?'*

Granted it was a mouthful. Not a particularly well-written mouthful. Yet not exactly unmemorizable. Instead of doing the job for which I was being ridiculously overpaid, I froze like Cindy Brady on that game show episode where she forgot Baton Rouge was the capital of Louisiana. 'Baton Rouge, Cindy! *Baton Rouge!'*[7]

If only I could have thrown some diva tantrum where I blamed the writers' absurdly humorless words, blamed the bad juju I was getting from the cast and crew, blamed the unsettling tantrum you'd thrown in my trailer. Anything would have been better than facing the truth: that I was just another insecure, untalented reality television star who had slept his way to a cushy primetime slot on Must See TV. Or at least that was the truth I assumed I was denying at the time.

Instead, during that particular take, during that particular scene, during that particular taping, while I was staring intently into the camera lens hovering in front of my face like a mosquito, I began to cry. And if that wasn't bad

---

[7] A classic *Brady Bunch* episode "Baton Rouge" escapes snotty Cindy after she wins a spot on "Quiz the Kids" over Bobby, whose own ego ruined his shot on the show.

enough, for the first time all night the paid laughers began to spontaneously laugh. For free.

Since I hadn't slept in days I'm not sure how much time had passed before one of the dwarves who stood in for one of the child actors attempted to comfort me by placing her little hand on my shoulder. She startled me and I accidentally threw my script, most likely at Camera Three, which may or may not have hit the cameraman, who assumed I had thrown it on purpose. The awkwardness, however, reached its crescendo when I realized I had scribbled my new dealer's new pager number was on the script's cover. I found myself in the precarious position of having to ask the poor guy to give it back. After that I skulked away, mortified.

IT WAS MY BIRTHDAY. Our birthday. Technically we had turned twenty-one at the stroke of midnight but you were on such a tweak that I'm not sure you realized. From your pungent odor that lingered long after you left my trailer, it was obvious you were well into one of your week long binges. The show was going on hiatus after we wrapped, perhaps permanently if the premiere tanked in the ratings, so it was extremely humiliating that nobody bothered to acknowledge it. Literally two days prior Craft Service had somehow pulled it together to make a cake (from scratch) for the beloved, yet horribly dyslexic Phone Page who never failed to invert numbers in everybody's phone messages. I felt like the Molly Ringwald character in *Sixteen Candles*. Except for the fact that she was a much better actor—an actor who could remember her lines, no less. But the icing on my missing cake? It had six goddamn more missing candles than Samantha Baker's. I was officially old. Or rather, we were.

And instead of Jake Ryan[8] sitting across the glass table from me as that old *Thompson Twins* song began to play, I was stuck with your voice berating me inside my head long after your tantrum had ended. *If you were here, I could deceive you. If you were here, you would believe…'*

I EXCUSED MYSELF from the hot Kitchen set and stretched out on the couch in the overly-lit Living Room set to look over my lines. That one hellish line in particular. That's when I noticed someone had left behind a forbidden copy of *The Hollywood Reporter,* even though my superstitious boyfriend had literally banned all trades from the set. I, of course, couldn't focus on my lines so I welcomed the distraction to review the critic's massacre of our imminent series premiere. I slyly inserted the paper rag into my script and angled myself away from the cameramen so my controversial act wouldn't be broadcast throughout the entire studio courtesy of the CCTV feed. I remember being instantly rattled by the unsettling cast photo that I still don't remember posing for.

Although my hazel eyes seemed to pop off the monochromatic page and my dimples gave me a slightly chiseled, bordering on starved look, I couldn't help think that the overly-tailored Helmut Lang suit made me look fat. Or was it Marc Jacobs? The brand didn't really matter. Nor did my ever increasing sense of body dysmorphia. All that mattered was the undisputed fact that the person in the photo staring back at me was an imposter. Like one of those chilly pod people from *Invasion of the Body Snatchers.*

---

[8] The quintessential Brat Pack movie, *Sixteen Candles* made Molly Ringwald a household name and unfortunately whomever played Jake Ryan, the popular yet sensitive high school athlete Molly Ringwald's character has a crush on, did not.

Even though my own fucking life had far surpassed my wildest, most narcissistic dreams, I knew in my heart that the pod person with the frosty smile and saucer-like pupils was anything but happy. He was a fraud. I took a long hard look at the black-and-white, Holden Caufield phony in the photograph and seriously began to wonder if perhaps you had been the one who posed for it?

I SHIVERED. From the air-conditioning, I told myself. But I decided to read the review, mostly to get my mind off the extremely unnerving, yet ironically complimentary photograph. The review was good. Too good. So goddamn good that I began to worry that I might actually deliver some of the effusive blurbs as dialog. Yet I was shocked and couldn't put it down. The reporter wrote about my fairy-tale relationship with Adam Roth, the *quote*, 'Emmy Award-winning, über-talented scribe who created and executive produced *Wall Street Widows*,' *unquote*. He droned on and on about how Adam had taken this huge gamble by leaving *Friends* to create a sitcom based around a *Doogie Houser* childhood has-been and a reality TV never-has whom Adam had, *quote*, 'hand-plucked from reality TV *Big Brother* fame,' *unquote*. Meanwhile all I remember thinking was, if my boyfriend was such a, *quote*, 'über-talented scribe,' *unquote*, then why couldn't he scribble, *quote*, 'Happy Birthday, Thom!' *unquote*, into a goddamn Hallmark card?'

I scanned the rest of the article, secretly hoping the show would get decimated and cancelled so I could sneak back to New York with my Hollywood tale held tight between my legs and retire from acting altogether. At the very least I expected the journalist to publically out me for my severe acting disability. But even *The Hollywood Reporter* didn't seem to be bothered by the fact that I couldn't act.

THE SOUNDSTAGE TEEMED with sleepwalking Teamsters as the double stage doors swung open and Mr. Über-Talent himself made an unscripted appearance from the exclusive control booth. Cast and crew synchronously dissolved out of Adam's way as if he were the Esther Williams[9] character in some overly-rehearsed Busby Berkeley[10] synchronized-swimming scene—Adam's toupee added to the whole effect since it lent him a certain swim-capish quality.

I knew I was the cause for concern but I just stared ambivalently into space as Adam and his production posse made a bee-line directly for me. He looked completely foreign. Kind of how a simple word can appear misspelled after you stare at it too long.

Anywhere else, like upscale shopping malls or hot new restaurants with unpublished phone numbers, I was the one who parted the red velvet ropes. Yet on the Universal Studios lot, specifically on Stage 6, Adam Roth was the Moses. Although the rest of the world would undoubtedly assume *Wall Street Widows* was my show, anyone who actually worked on it knew that it was indeed Adam Roth who gaveth, and Adam Roth who re-wroteth away.

---

[9] Esther Williams is a retired American competitive swimmer and MGM movie star who made a series of films in the 1940s and early 1950s known as "aquamusicals", featuring elaborate performances with synchronized swimming and diving.
[10] Busby Berkeley was a highly influential Hollywood movie director and musical choreographer, famous for his elaborate musical production numbers that often involved complex geometric patterns. The combination of these two references in one sentence is perhaps the gayest thing ever said since the dawn of gay man. Definitely a Kinsey 6. Possible even a 7.

His dictatorial power commanded this disturbing, yet pervasive, ass-kissy affection that was really quite astonishing. Adam's Hollywood hostages would relentlessly show their undying loyalty to their entertainment industry abductor as if they were suffering from some psychotic studio strain of the Stockholm Syndrome. However they personally felt about Adam, publicly the cast and crew worshiped the ground he walked on. Everybody assured him that his schlocky new show would be a gigantic hit. Everybody blew Hollywood smog up his ass. Everybody but me. And that's probably why he was attracted to me in the first place.

I REMEMBER BEING struck by a plummeting feeling of distance when Adam and his not-so-merry minions marched over to console me for my teary televised outburst. Adam was standing so intimidatingly close that the heat from his coffee breath felt like he was giving me mouth-to-mouth, yet somehow I still felt like I was drowning. Instead of throwing me a life preserver, or even a simple 'Happy Birthday,' Adam cleared his throat as well his stragglers with one simple, callous command, 'Give us a minute.'

Any hope of empathy disappeared as quickly as Adam's posse of Yes Men. They receded into a tight huddle of tailored suits and designer nose jobs and most likely complained about the pitfalls of hiring a young Reality TV star for a scripted show. Especially one who couldn't act.

In a hushed, yet piercing tone, Adam demanded answers from me, 'Why the hell did you break into tears like that? On camera? In front of Studio Execs who fought me tooth and nail when I wanted to cast you in the show?'

'I'm sorry,' I lied.

'If you had a problem with your dialog then I don't know why I'm first hearing about it midnight on the longest Tape day since the dawn of gay sitcom.'

'You're hearing about it because my character would never talk like this,' I shook my script for effect and the banned copy of *The Hollywood Reporter* fell out and plopped onto Adam's shiny new Gucci's like unexpected bird shit falling from the sky.

Adam laughed patronizingly, 'I created your character! He says whatever I want him to say!' I rolled my eyes as he asked, 'Are you done sabotaging your career yet?'

Apparently I wasn't because I was totally tripping over whether Adam was in actually in love with me or the two-dimensional caricature he had created on paper? That's when I asked, in a tone that came out way too earnest, 'Why do you always have to be in control of everything?'

Adam stared at me quietly, eerily, as I slipped deeper into my own oral quicksand, 'Is that why you wanted me to be in your show? So you'd have control of each and every word that came out of my mouth?'

Adam threw his arms up in disgust as he looked up to an imaginary Judge, 'And that's when I shot him, Your Honor.'

'My character might say something like that.'

Then there was another unsettling pause. Even though I was significantly taller, Adam seemed to hover above me like a Charlie Brown parent or a gigantic helium float in the Macy's Thanksgiving Day Parade. He stared intently as if he was on the brink of solving my elusive riddle. My eyes darted around uncomfortably in an attempt to avoid his overly attentive gaze. I definitely wasn't ready to be figured out, yet I was even less prepared when he inquired in a hushed tone, 'Are you high?'

Since I couldn't actually remember when I had begun that particular binge, or the last time I hadn't been high, or the last time I slept for that matter, my pupils instinctively ducked for cover as I vehemently denied his accusation, 'Absolutely not.' It was truly, by leaps and bounds, the best acting I'd done all night.

FLASHBACK TO being a contestant on *Big Brother*. Had I known it would've done so much irreparable damage to my relationship with you, I never would've applied. Forget the fact that it I didn't actually apply. You were the one who was dying to be on a damn reality show. You wanted to be discovered. Needed to be. I remember chuckling when you told me that reality shows were the Hollywood drugstore fountains of the twenty-first century. Ironically, the joke was on me.

Even though most people find it impossible to tell identical twins apart, for some unknown reason I was the one who CBS chose to audition from the video we made together. This, of course, did nothing to help our increasingly awkward relationship. From your point of view, it was very *All About Eve*.[11] But from my P.O.V. it was simply a way to escape you with the bonus chance of winning a half million dollars.

Although you disappeared on a regular basis, it was the first time I'd ever chosen to leave you. At twenty years old I found myself reveling in the idea of spending a summer locked away in a fake house that you weren't allowed to visit. A place you couldn't call, email, or even send a goddamn emotionally abusive fax. No matter how awful the *Big Brother* contestants were, the experience was an

[11] *All About Eve* is a 1950 American drama film starring Bette Davis as Margo Channing, a highly regarded but aging Broadway star. Anne Baxter plays Eve Harrington, a willingly helpful young fan who insinuates herself into Channing's life, ultimately stealing Channing's career and her personal relationships. If you had to read this, shame on you. Just watch it already.

upgrade from living with you in squalor in our sixth-floor, Hell's Kitchen walkup. It was a place that I could exist without you. Where nobody would judge me because they knew I was related to you. Where nobody would know you existed unless I expressly told them. Needless to say I jumped at the opportunity. Partly to spite you, but mostly because my being on television meant that I could escape you. And I never once mentioned your name to anyone on the show, not even in the diary room. It was like you didn't exist. And I loved it.

UNLIKE YOU, I never had any desire to be a celebrity. At all. Although I didn't win *Big Brother*, I lasted in the house long enough that I could barely walk down the street without being recognized by some stranger who yapped my ear off. Most people think that kind of celebrity crap is cool, but most people can't imagine being totally hungover, minding their own business when some random, fanny pack-wearing tourist on Hollywood Boulevard starts to blah-blah-blah all about Julie Chen's eating disorder and seriously questioning me about whether or not she had bulimia breath.[12]

Strangers felt like they knew who I was solely because I was on television. I told myself that fame hadn't changed me, that fame had only changed the way the world perceived me. The ironic part was that, in the scheme of things, I was barely famous. A fact that you reveled in reminding me.

---

[12] Julie Chen is an American television personality, news anchor, and producer for CBS. The Chenbot has hosted *Big Brother* since its debut in July 2000 and is the longest-serving host of any country's version of the show. She is also the thinnest.

I HAD NO PLACE to go after the show ended since you had legally sublet our illegal tenement apartment and then disappeared. Again. I certainly wasn't about to ask our certifiably insane pill-head of a mother for help. What was the point? Forget about the fact that she hated us, probably because we were gay. Mommie Dearest was obviously living on fumes, and the idea of leaving LA to move back to Connecticut and live in our dilapidated Home-Sweet-Hovel was absolutely out of the question. I hadn't spoken to Mother since I dropped out of Bennington. The only reason I even applied to that ridiculous school in the first place was because I had some silly teenaged fantasy about being the next Bret Easton Ellis. Ironically the only thing remotely *Less Than Zero* about my college experience was my freshman year's G.P.A. Now I just tell people I graduated from Camden.[13] Nobody ever bats an eye.

I WAS JUST LIKE EVERYONE else in LA. Good looking enough, young enough, and ridiculously naive enough not to realize that I was just like everyone else in LA. I was penniless with nothing but a pedigree of questionable breeding, a fictional education and ridiculously good luck. Although it was my first trip to California, I didn't feel anything like Mary Ann Singleton seeing San Francisco for the first time. Partly because Los Angeles was one big strip mall with valet parking, but mostly because, after being a contestant on *Big Brother,* strangers began to look at me suspiciously like I was some Norman Neal Williams creeping around 28 Barbary Lane.[14]

---

[13] Camden is a fictional New England college in Bret Easton Ellis' debut novel *Less Than Zero,* loosely based on his alma mater, Bennington College. If the movie was as loosely based on the book, it might have been watchable.

As usual, you appeared out of nowhere one day when I was living in some flea ridden Hollywood hooker hotel on maxed out credit cards. Even after a month on the *Big Brother* peanut-butter-and-jelly diet, you were somehow thinner than me. Your face had actually sunk to the point where your eyes appeared larger than life with a slightly sad quality, kind of like Japanese anime with AIDS. I'd be lying if I didn't say it was shocking, but I assumed you were on some silly Jenny Crank actor diet.

You claimed you had come to Los Angeles for Pilot Season. Whoever said L.A. had no seasons obviously never worked in television. Instead of falling leaves, once a year Hollywood Boulevard becomes littered with fallen actors who descend upon the left coast for that none-in-a-million chance to be cast in a new pilot.

When I asked about auditions, you were beyond vague. And that sleazy old guy who gave you your own wing in his sprawling house seemed more like your pimp than your manager. Like most everything else in your life, when pressed for details about your Pimp-ager, you refused to elaborate. But after you invited me to move in with you, I stopped pressing.

YOUR PECULIAR BEHAVIOR never made sense until you reluctantly took me to that New Year's party in the Hollywood Hills. The one thrown by some obscure Aussie actor named after an English toffee bar. Heath something or other. He was only our age but had already starred in a few movies, mostly unwatchable.

---

[14] One of the beloved characters in Armistead Maupin's series of novels, *Tales of the City*, Mary Ann Singleton is a naive young woman from Cleveland, Ohio, who went on vacation to San Francisco and impulsively decides to stay. Norman Neal Williams is the sinister and cagey neighbor who she pity-dates before realizing he dabbles in child pornography.

He was dating that Rollergirl from *Boogie Nights,* even though she was way too old for him—thirtysomething if she was a day.

The party was intimidating. We ordered drinks at the open bar and then you quickly abandoned me as well as your Cosmo, disappearing long before the bartender finished shaking it. The fact that you ditched me didn't make much sense since my only goal was to help you network. I tagged along with the hope that my newfound, half-assed celebrity might open doors and help you book a legitimate acting gig.

I found myself wandering around aimlessly, trying desperately to make small talk. All those actors in one place did nothing but create this giant black hole of narcissism which sucked away at my already non-existent self-esteem. I felt like some unworthy, no-talent imposter who was singlehandedly responsible for the reality TV craze which was taking imaginary acting jobs away from delusional waiters. You, of course, fit right in.

I spent most of the night searching for you all over the Rat Packy, mid-century rental house which was overflowing with Brat Packy, east-of-Western Avenue hipsters. Eventually my quest led me into a basement sauna (which thankfully hadn't been turned on), and I found some bald guy with an unfortunate toupee muttering to himself as he rhythmically chopped up lines on some retro, starburst-shaped, antique mirror that had been yanked off the starburst-stained wall. His antisocial, bordering-on-selfish behavior suddenly made complete sense, yet I couldn't stop myself from joining his party of one. 'How much of that have you done?'

The Rug shot back, 'Not nearly enough!' and laid out four of the fattest lines I'd ever seen. He held up the mirror and showed his line art off to me with exotic hand gestures before handing me the mirror like he was one of those aging blondes on *The Price Is Right*. It was the nicest anyone had been to me in months, possibly years, and I felt like it would be rude to turn down the stranger's generous offer.

I IMMEDIATELY FELL to my knees, screaming in pain, feeling like my nose was bleeding because the coke I'd inhaled had obviously been cut with tiny shards of glass. My mind was racing as fast as my heart when I screeched, 'What the fuck is that coke cut with?'

The Rug chuckled and nonchalantly informed me, 'It's not coke,' which became immediately apparent when I looked back down at the mirror, a bit more suspiciously, and realized that it didn't even look like coke. It never crossed my mind that it'd be anything else, that some stranger would offer me crystal meth without bothering to mention it.

Even though the pain was excruciating, the instantaneous euphoria was equally exhilarating. It was unlike anything I'd ever felt before. I greedily accepted the second line, lying to you with some nonsense about how it probably made sense for me to even out the pain in my nostrils.

The Rug was obviously tweaking when he recognized me, 'Wait a minute, I know you! I'm a total *Big Brother* fanatic!'

I wasn't about to waste my newfound high answering The Rug's irritating questions about my irritating housemates on *Big Brother*, so I quickly told him that he must have mistaken me for you before I escaped back into the swarm of irritating actors who suddenly became a lot less irritating.

In fact, it quickly turned out to be the best party I'd ever been to. The best night I'd ever had. I'd never been particularly good with other people. I was awkward at best and usually came off aloof, bordering on standoffish. Yet at that party, teeming with famous people, I felt more secure than Linus, warmly wrapped up like a mummy in his security blanket. I was funny. Vivacious, even. The life of the fucking party. For the first time in my life I wasn't scared to say what was on my mind. I didn't care what people thought. Not even you. I felt powerful. Confident. From that moment on, it was all about me. I was the 'King of the World' and everybody else was just a non-featured extra on my sinking ship.

THE NEXT DAY I still hadn't slept. Perhaps it had been two days? You were still out partying as I was scanning through your extensive collection of porn DVDs, looking for something to draw my attention, keep my attention, when I stumbled upon Rod Hard, the gay porn actor formerly known as you.

The video was shocking. Somehow you were lying on your back, on top of this cheesy orange oil drum that literally had the misspelled words, 'Oil Durm,' stenciled on its side. An insanely hairy leather daddy, bearded, dripping in tattoos, veiny, splotchy, most likely HIV positive, was holding your legs by the ankles, up in the air, spread eagle, fucking you without a condom as you moaned repeatedly, 'Breed me.'

You squealed with pleasure when the hairy guy shoved some huge funnel up your ass and proceeded to pour an entire can of crude inside you. Although it was probably Hershey's chocolate syrup, it was beyond disconcerting when you began to expel your black tar enema all over the hairy guy, in what can only described as a disturbing diarrhea effect.

I WAS JERKING OFF when that call came through on your creepy manager's landline. From that casting director. April something. Named after a dictionary, I think.

April Dictionary told me she was casting *The Untitled Neil Patrick Harris Project* and that Adam Roth had told her to bring me in. After my awkward hesitation followed by her hefty sigh, April Dictionary informed me that Adam was an Executive Producer whom I'd allegedly met at the New Year's party. I racked my brain trying to remember meeting anyone named Adam. Naturally, I blamed Blackout Barbie for paying me another unwelcomed visit, yet did my best to pretend I knew exactly who the casting director was talking about.

When you finally returned home after the New Year's party, two days into the new year, all you wanted to do was crash, and all I wanted to do was tell you my good news, but all your sleazy old Pimpager wanted to do was to fuck you. Needless to say, it was the perfect Hollywood storm which, unbeknownst to me, had been brewing for months.

I was busy rehearsing sides that April Dictionary had faxed over, but took a break to eavesdrop while your Pimpager interrogated you, following you around his house in the same way that Mommie Dearest had just before she kicked you out for good, 'Where on earth have you been?'

You rolled your eyes, 'I told you, I went to a New Year's party.'

'You told me that back in 2000. It's now 2001 and I was worried.'

'Did you call the cops?'

'No.'

'Then you obviously weren't that worried.'

You opened the guestroom door, but just stood there, staring him down, daring him to probe further into your private affairs. It was obvious that your Pimpager was at his wits end as I had seen the lost look in his eyes many times before. He hesitated in the doorjamb for a moment, before interjecting, 'Did you hear the good news?'

'What good news?'

'There's a message on the machine,' he smirked in a pot-stirring kind of way, then left us alone in anything but peace.

You raced over to the answering machine and played the message from April Dictionary, ignoring me as if I wasn't standing there, watching you, listening over your shoulder. Afterward the message played you just stood there for a long beat before you turned around and scared the smile off my face with what had become your signature scowl.

'What? You don't think that's amazing?'

'Oh it's beyond amazing. Do you even know who Adam Roth is?'

'Of course. He's the executive producer of *The Untitled Doogie Howser Project.*'

'He was the guy in the sauna!'

I said, 'He was?' And then I was confused, 'How would you know? You weren't even there.'

You screamed, 'Of course I was there!' then yanked the answering machine from the wall and threw it at me, narrowly missing my head by inches.

It was exactly the way you reacted when they cast me on *Big Brother*, 'Don't be jealous.'

'Jealous? Of *you?!* You're not even the one who booked the fucking audition! Who do you think I've been with the last two nights?' Venom dripped from your fangs as I cowered in the corner, unsure of what you might do next. As usual, your erratic course of action took me completely by surprise.

You grabbed the largest suitcase from the closet and haphazardly dumped your clothes into it, silently, violently, drawer by drawer. You paused briefly while staring into the last drawer, then removed a wad of colorful eight-by-tens and threw them into the air like confetti. Your headshots hadn't even settled on the floor before you zipped up the bag and rolled it away.

It wasn't until I saw the name beneath your photograph, *my* name, that I had realized what you had done. I hadn't blacked out anything. Adam Roth didn't want to meet me and April Dictionary was definitely not calling for me. She was calling for you. All of a sudden it became clear that you had been parading around Los Angeles all these months, going to pretentious parties, meeting with C.A.A. agents, going on random auditions, pretending you were the one who had been on *Big Brother*, using my name to get auditions. It'd been so long since we had played the identity-swap game that it had never even crossed my mind that it was still in the realm of possibility.

What would you have done had you gotten the job? Did you think I wouldn't notice that I was somehow miraculously starring in a sitcom that I'd never auditioned for? The most astonishing aspect of the whole ludicrous situation was that you were the one who got mad. Livid, actually. To my surprise, however, I had grown a long lost backbone, or more likely snorted one, and for once I wasn't going to let you steamroll me. For the first time in my life I actually stood up to your constant stream of demeaning bullshit. I decided right then and there that I would pull a *Victor/Victoria* and pretend to be you pretending to be me and go to the goddamn audition. Partly to spite you, but mostly so I could make sure that you didn't show up and make-believe you were me. Again.

DISSOLVE TO a lovely montage of me auditioning for a cameo in *The Untitled Neil Patrick Harris Project* where I realized that Adam Roth and The Rug were one and the same. When I booked the job I only had four one-syllable words in one absurdly unnecessary scene that was destined for the cutting room floor, but for some unknown reason the network thought that Neil Patrick Harris and I had chemistry. Whereas it was obvious that Neil Patrick Harris and Danny Pintauro had none. Everybody loved my newfound, boundless energy. Especially Adam Roth who was directly responsible for it. My cameo was expanded. Twice. By the time the Writers Run-Thru happened, my Featured Extra role had been upgraded to Special Guest Star. And since Danny Pintauro hadn't done anything since *Who's The Boss,* and since the pilot was definitely not *The Untitled Danny Pintauro Project,* and since *Big Brother* had turned into a sleeper hit that summer, and since the network actually thought I had more TV-Q than Danny, NBC approached my B-list New York Reality TV agent about an A-list recurring role. The contractual discussions with Danny Pintauro's agent got so heated that the network asked me to re-create all of Danny's previously recorded pilot scenes, effectively erasing his existence from the entire project. I actually liked working with the poor guy. But now Danny hates me, too. Ironically, he probably hates me more than anyone. Except for you.

FLASH FORWARD to the taping on the frigid soundstage. I had absolutely no clue how to react when Adam confronted me about tweaking since I had long ago promised that I wouldn't mix show business with pleasure. Drugs were for weekends, holidays and hiatuses. Of course

I justified using because it helped me focus, doing lines helped me remember lines, helped boost my confidence, helped my comedic timing. It was a win-win situation for everybody. After all, I was acting, not operating heavy machinery.

Meanwhile, there I was, fucking up my lines, costing the studio a fortune in crew overtime, so I decided it was in my best interest to keep my mouth busy doing something other than argue my losing case. I reflexively guzzled an entire bottle of Evian, partly to hydrate, but mostly so I couldn't accidentally speak to Adam and dig myself in further. While I was sipping water from the bottle the silence on the soundstage was unbearable. The only noise came from my guilty gulps, but ultimately the stillness was interrupted by the Director's disembodied voice which echoed over the public address system from the control booth, 'Are you ready to try this again, Thom?'

Besides the fact that I was too nervous to speak, my jaw was clenched shut, grinding away, so I resorted to nodding at the Director through Camera Two's lens and a nanosecond later the Assistant Director shouted, 'Okay, people, let's get this last scene in the can so we can all go home and get some sleep! Places everyone!' Adam walked quietly back to the control booth, shaking of his head with deafening disapproval.

In anticipation of the umpteenth take of the endless scene, the Sound Department shut off the overworked A/C and the Key Grip turned up the surrounding floodlights to their full wattage. Since our show had no budget due to the gay 'issue,' it was being shot on tape instead of film and the cinematography experience could only be described as retinal rape. Blinded, I squeezed my feet back into their leather Prada torture devices so my blisters and I could painfully saunter over to our mark by the refrigerator. As usual, The Writers buzzed around The

Suits like flies swarming around a cow's ass, telling lame jokes to keep them in a jovial mood (even though it was approaching 10pm and everyone's mood ring had long since turned jet black).

I remember how late it was because I was completely shocked when I saw it illuminated on the vibrating Motorola StarTAC I'd been given in an overflowing swag bad during the New York Upfronts. I found it extremely bizarre that someone would be calling me during the taping. At first I worried that it was security calling about something questionable you had done, and then I hoped it was from my elusive dealer returning my last page, yet I was ultimately freaked when the Caller ID informed me that it was 'Do Not Answer' calling. Again. That's how I had him programmed into my cell. Even though 'Do Not Answer' was probably the only person on earth who had actually remembered to wish me happy birthday, I instinctively banished my stalker to voicemail. Remember that time you told me that the one thing that made him absolutely, certifiably insane, was the fact that he had chosen to stalk me? It was hard to believe that you could be jealous of the fact that I had a stalker, yet utterly predictable.

THE FIRST TIME he called he seemed harmless. It was right after the live *Big Brother* finale, at which point I was totally unaccustomed to receiving unsolicited attention from strangers. Now I don't even blink when someone stops to stare. Like when I'm walking through a parking lot. Or standing at a urinal. I can almost see the cogs churning in their heads as they try to figure out how they know me. One guy thought he remembered me from Gay Traffic School in Sherman Oaks. Another was absolutely positive that I was her nephew who got soaked during the water balloon toss at the annual Zinn cousins' party. My favorite instance of mistaken identity, however, was the GoGo boy at some insanely raunchy East Village underwear party at The Slide. He was hanging from a sprinkler pipe, totally naked, staring at me, saucer-eyed, as if I was the one making a spectacle of myself. Eventually, the GoGo turned to me while some dirty old party promoter named Daniel Narcissist was literally fingering the teenager's ass. The GoGo asked me, nonchalantly, 'Didn't you take my sister Doris to the Lower Merion junior prom?'

But back when 'Do Not Answer' began to stalk me, nobody even knew who I was—let alone cared. He caught me totally off guard. The second time he called I think I was couch surfing on Avenue B for someone who had Hepatitis C. Possibly vice versa. Anyway. I was way over my monthly allotment of minutes so I didn't answer, which was a good thing since he totally rambled during his voicemail and never got to the point. He sounded medicated. Possibly drunk. And like most drunks he came off surprisingly earnest, like he wasn't full of shit. In his message he yapped about how he used to know me back when I was a little boy, about how it was his biggest regret in life that we had lost touch. He sounded creepy, like a child molester rattling off detailed crap that only crazy people feel comfortable saying aloud.

The guy kept calling. Leaving messages. He began to freak me out. Especially after that one particularly disturbing voicemail. The one where he claimed to be our father. My first response was some wishful thinking, that perhaps we had been adopted, that maybe we had no direct DNA connection to Mommie Dearest and possibly my deranged fan was our long-lost birthfather who had no choice in the matter of putting us up for adoption. Perhaps he was trying to track me down for some tearful Oprah reunion where everybody in the studio audience gets a gift bag with their own personal box of Kleenex.

He really pulled at my heartstrings in that voicemail and I even considered calling him back until the freak finally broke down and gave me his full name. That's when I knew I was being taken for a ride. That it was some sick, twisted joke. I remember getting insanely angry when he finally identified himself, 'It's your father. Thom Thompson, Jr.'

The fact that there had been not one, but two fathers besides mine who had the sick sense of humor to condemn their sons to go through life with a ridiculously repetitive name like Thompson Thompson was beyond me. But I digress.

From that point on I began to delete my Stalker's messages without listening to them. It was just too upsetting to dredge up the memory of Daddy's casket being lowered into the earth every time the nut-job left a message . By that time you had already abandoned me for pilot season in L.A. but I remember leaving you frantic a voicemail about how I was freaked out over the whole fucked up situation. You, of course, took two days to respond to my panicked voicemail with something lame and completely cryptic like, 'i thought he wuz dead.' Via text message, no less. The annoying way you spelled 'wuz' was the least irritating thing about your response.

At the time I wanted nothing to do with some freak who was pretending to be, or even worse, actually believed that he was our dead father. When I told Adam about my stalker he told me to get a restraining order. I thought about changing my number, but worried about alienating my dealers. Eventually the messages petered out and I forgot about them. But now that I was on a new show that was being heavily promoted by the network, 'Do Not

Answer' was back. My knee-jerk reaction was to tell Adam about my stalker's resurrection, but I was too paranoid to give him any opportunity to inspect my pupils. I was also more than a little pissed that he forgot my birthday.

I banished my stalker to voicemail, walked off set and began to run around the stage, frantically looking for you. Everyone kept asking me if something was wrong, but I said everything was fine. The idea of explaining that I had a brother, let alone a twin, seemed much too time consuming. Although my denial of you may have begun on *Big Brother* as a way to hurt you, I quickly realized how liberating it was to be my own person and I had no misgivings. I never even told Adam that he had accidentally slept with you. But that's another story altogether which ultimately doesn't matter because I desperately needed you to give me another bump so I could pull it together and get through the rest of the damn scene. I finally tracked you down in my trailer, hiding from the government while obsessively sorting a giant bowl of M&M's. First by color, then by size.

I DID A FEW BUMPS and then, since you were terrified to leave the trailer regardless of how many times I assured you the government helicopters were nowhere to be found, I tuned the television channel to the camera feed so you could watch the show, so you would watch me do exactly what you so desperately wanted to be doing. It was cruel, but if anyone deserved to wallow in my success it was you.

The stage was buzzing almost as much as I was when I returned to the set after my extended 'diva' absence. My heart was racing so fast that I had to do the breathing exercises you had taught me to slow it down. My body shivered mechanically as I passed by a sign that read 'Hot Set.' I stood quietly on my mark which was literally just some crisscrossed black tape on some linoleum floor designed to look like hardwood. I took one last glance at the previously unmemorizable, highlighted line and instantly burned it into memory as if I'd taken a Polaroid. My elusive confidence had finally returned and I was confident we could easily finish the last scene. In one take. Maybe less.

When Adam asked me patronizingly over the PA system, 'Are we ready now?' *we* didn't answer because, as you know, it thoroughly annoys *us* when people use the royal *we* when they really mean *me*. It's obviously a twin thing. Regardless, *we* ignored Adam until he finally punctuated *our* passive-aggressive question with an actual non-plural subject, '...Thom?'

I turned toward Camera Three and gave my best clueless look as I said confidently, 'Oh. I had no idea you meant *me*. Yes, of course *we're* ready,' as if *we* hadn't just broken into unscripted weeping ten minutes prior, possibly thirty. Then I crumpled my Evian bottle and handed the plastic carcass to my assistant along with my highlighted shooting script that had my new dealer's new pager number scrawled on the cover.

'ACTION!'

I swung open the door of the stainless steel SubZero and reached into the non-working freezer. Ironically, the fridge was considerably warmer than the icy soundstage since it was really just a giant prop that couldn't be turned on as the compressor made too much noise for the Sound Department's liking.

I pretended to pick through the fake frozen food before removing my business, which, in that particular scene happened to be a fake frosty bottle of Grey Goose. I remember wishing it was real because I desperately needed to even out. I was beyond jumpy when I walked over to the counter and poured several, non-alcoholic gaggles of grey geese into two supersized Martini glasses.

I found myself back in the familiar showdown between my feeble short-term memory and the heckling red light above Camera One, but thanks to your generosity I was no longer saddled by the debilitating fear that I'd forgotten my lines and the previously elusive dialog miraculously began to spew from my mouth like poorly written puke. 'If something unpleasant happens on Wall Street and there are no inside traders around to initiate a sell-off, does it really happen?'

We were doing a riff on George and Martha from *Who's Afraid of Virginia Woolf?*[15] and Neil Patrick Harris sat on a barstool, equally shocked as I was that I'd finally spit out that goddamn line. He flipped through an oversized copy of *Vogue Hommes* and graciously accepted the Martini mocktail I handed him. Then, without spilling a drop or moving a single facial muscle, Neil clinked my glass and channeled his inner-Jan Brady for his next line, even though he ended up sounding more like a lisping Cindy,[16]

---

[15] *Who's Afraid of Virginia Woolf?* is a 1966 film based on an adaptation of the play by Edward Albee. It stars Richard Burton as George and Elizabeth Taylor as his hard-drinking wife, Martha. The film was nominated for thirteen Academy Awards and remains the only film to be nominated in every eligible category at the Academy Awards. Put it in your Netflix queue now.

[16] *The Brady Bunch* episode entitled "Her Sister's Shadow" centers around middle sister Jan who is fed up with her perfect sister that she whines "Marsha, Marsha, Marsha!" The famous line, however, didn't go viral until Melanie Hutsell literally channeled Eve Plumb on the 17th season of Saturday Night Live. YouTube it now if you know what's good for you.

'Martha, Martha, Martha! If we could marry, I'd divorce you.' The ImClone Martha Stewart reference was totally lame but it was a callback to an earlier, slightly less lame joke and got a big, fake guffaw from a few Paid Laughers who pretended they hadn't already heard it a thousand times during rehearsal.

The laugh was my cue to take a big gulp from my mocktail in order to prepare for a scripted spit-take, but that's when, from the corner of my eye, I saw the vague black blur swoop down from the rafters, seemingly out of nowhere. Although the attack was obviously random, at the time it felt personal, like a Japanese kamikaze pilot mistaking me for Pearl Harbor. Several black crows had been featured in the previous week's episode, and evidently one of the trained birds had gone M.I.A. while nesting in the rafters all week. Waiting. Obviously it was back with a vengeance, clearly blaming me for being trapped in its cavernous soundstage-cage all week.

The next part's a bit hazy because after I realized I was literally being dive-bombed by a bird of prey, smack in the middle of Neil's monologue, I ended up throwing my martini glass to protect myself and dove for cover beneath the kitchen island's marble countertop. While I was hiding I vaguely remember hearing some actual unrehearsed, yet extremely uncomfortable laughter fill the soundstage. Possibly gasps. Other than that it was eerily silent. Even the Extras were speechless, and they never shut up except for those ironically brief moments when they were actually on camera.

There were a few hushed beats before Neil's unforgettable shriek. It sounded like he was Tippi Hedren auditioning for a Hitchcock movie, most likely *The Birds*.[17]

---

[17] Hitchcock directed Hedren in her debut film, *The Birds*. For the final attack scene in a second-floor bedroom, Hedren endured five solid days of prop men, protected by thick leather gloves, flinging dozens of live gulls, ravens

By the time I emerged from my hiding place, blood was gushing down Neil's mangled face. I was shocked by how badly the crow had gouged him. I remember thinking that he was lucky that the bird had missed his eye. Department heads from Hair, Makeup and Wardrobe leapt into frame and dragged Neil away before the Director had a chance to yell, 'Cut!'

I looked toward the rafters, paranoid that the vindictive crow might make another attack while asking repeatedly, 'Where did it go? Where the fuck did it go?' Everyone kept backing away from me. Uncomfortable. Silent. Ultimately Adam emerged from the control booth, pulled me aside and asked, quite gravely, 'Why did you throw your martini at Neil's face?'

'Are you kidding?' was all I could muster. He obviously hadn't even seen the evil bird from the camera's vantage point. No one had seen it. My eyes scanned the soundstage, partly because I needed to prove to Adam that I wasn't crazy, but mostly because I was terrified that it might dive-bomb us again. Its whereabouts didn't matter much since as far as everybody else was concerned, I was the one who had mauled my co-star's face. Had the cocktail merely ruined his wardrobe or makeup, everything would've been fine; something to laugh about after the taping. But, allegedly, my oversized martini glass ended up shattering in Neil Patrick Harris's face.

The Director made an announcement over the P.A. system telling everybody to 'Take five.' Sweat oozed through pores which had recently been frozen shut as I chased after Neil to make sure he was okay. I wanted to apologize and make sure he knew about the bird. Needed to. Adam had an arm over my co-star's shoulder as he

---

and crows at her (their beaks clamped shut with elastic bands). In a state of exhaustion, when one of the birds gouged her cheek and narrowly missed her eye, Hedren sat down on the set and began crying.

escorted him toward the stage door. Toward safety. Away from that evil crow. Away from me.

I chased them through the stage door and raced outside to catch up to my wounded co-star. And that's when I saw it. Parked in my assigned parking place. Next to one of the enormous pop-outs on my oversized trailer. The exact spot where I'd parked my boring beige Budget rental when I had arrived at the studio that particular morning. I was shocked that I had somehow not noticed it earlier since I had been back and forth a dozen times, mostly to snort in private. That's when I began to worry that I had lost control of my tweak because it seemed impossible to miss the gargantuan white ribbon tied to the hood of a brand new, fire-engine red Porsche 911 Carrera Cabriolet.

ONCE UPON A TIME, most likely when I was tweaking, I must have told Adam the story about Daddy's Porsche. About how we used to call it the Nine-One-One since neither of us could pronounce 'eleven.' About how Mommie Dearest had chained it to the chestnut tree years after she had driven her own Audi into the swimming pool while *accidentally* murdering Daddy. About how, one day, it was my life's dream to free it from its prison. Or at the very least, have a Porsche of my own.

I found myself semi-confused when Adam confirmed my suspicion. He said more than a bit sarcastically, 'Happy birthday, Thom!' as he blotted Neil Patrick Harris's gouged forehead with the corner of an enormous white ribbon that he yanked from the 911's hood. In lieu of thanking Adam, I apologized profusely for assuming he had forgotten my birthday. He said, *'That's* what you're apologizing for?' Adam just shook his head before he drove off to take Neil to see his personal plastic surgeon instead of letting an E.R. doctor botch him up.

I don't know how long I stood there, admiring the beautiful car. Eventually I went to back to my trailer to collect you, but as usual, you had disappeared. Since it was my birthday, our birthday, instead of popping the usual Ambien with a Xanax chaser to ease the inevitable crash after a long taping, I amped it up a bit and did a few bumps before heading over to The Abbey[18] to celebrate the last few hours of that 10th day of September.

---

[18] The Abbey was *the* bar and nightclub in West Hollywood, California for A-list gays and D-list celebrities.

8

THE ABBEY WAS BUZZING with fags and their hags when the out-of-work actress who had recently gotten a callback for a Geico commercial asked if I'd like to order another round. I blurted out, 'Let them have cocktails!' Although it didn't make me feel any better, all the drunks within earshot were certainly grateful, which was pretty much the entire bar since the gays in Los Angeles never stray too far if there's a celebrity to gawk.

The fact that I was wearing the 'Fuck Me I'm Famous' t-shirt you gave me didn't help my anonymity much. I was convinced that you only bought it for me as an obnoxious attempt to make me feel bad about myself, but I totally loved that shirt. Probably because you had given it to me. Possibly because I knew it was a snarky gift since you were truly jealous of my fame. But the really ironic part was that it was getting harder to wear the ironic T without any sense of irony. Anyway.

Other out-of-work gay actors who weren't currently working a shift at The Abbey were networking around the vast bar as if they were seeking representation in a perfectly choreographed dance. The constant spew of disjointed conversations began to meld together in my mind as my attention deficit drifted in and out like the tide affected by a full bar. One moment I was being hit on by some Featured Extra with a recurring role as a Personal Trainer at the Sports Erection in WeHo, and the next I'd be drifting back out to sea, protecting my eyes from the disturbingly white teeth of a 5' 5" Under-Five[19] from *The*

Young and The Restless. Trapped, I had no choice but to drown myself in another frothy pink Cosmopolitan to help even out my tweak.

WHEN THE 80 PROOF lunar tide finally washed me back onto The Abbey's shore, I found myself having the same exact tête-à-tête with some corn-fed, bottle blond homosexual who couldn't seem to construct a sentence without compulsively lisping about his fiancé—allegedly female. The Gay Fiancé droned on and on about some yet-to-be-released, presumably no-budget indie movie called *Camp,* in which he starred. He yapped about how he drank bug juice on the set with Stephen Sondheim but, surprise-surprise, his real dream, hint-hint, was to be cast in a sitcom. Although he was extremely cute and I was extremely horny, my attention turned to pity when he handed me his so-called business card which was printed on an ink jet using perforated card stock. His occupation was listed as 'Actor.' In quotes, no less. I felt sad for the Gay Fiancé who continued to drone on, but it wasn't long before I found myself doing the L.A. scan, browsing the endless sea of out-of-work actors for one who didn't put amateurish 'quotes' around his 'profession.'

My SOS call was answered in the form of a rescue ring, or more specifically, the vibration emanating from my denim pocket. Unfortunately, my incessant phone phobia had been on high alert ever since 'Do Not Answer' had called. Since I didn't recognize the random (310) number, I decided it was best not to answer. Yet when the message finally beeped through, I politely excused myself and hoped the Gay Fiancé would get the hint and move on

---

[19] An Under-Five is an AFTRA-only contract term for an American soap opera actor whose character has under five lines of dialogue in an episode

while I listened to my voicemail. He, of course, was even more polite and waited patiently.

The random (310) number turned out to be this bizarre message from Adam, 'Where the hell are you? I told you we needed to hide out here until things blow over. As soon as this news hits it's gonna be a shit storm.'

I heard an anxious knock on the door and then Adam said, 'Oh good, this better be you.' Then Adam threw the receiver down but the phone didn't hang up. In the background he said, 'Where the hell have you been? I was just leaving you a message.'

I almost threw up when I heard your voice answer, 'I scored some more tweak.' I wanted to hang up, but couldn't bring myself to disengage.

Adam told you, 'I have some very bad news,' because he thought he was telling me.

It wasn't long before it got quiet. Much, much too quiet.

And then after what felt like an eternity Adam finally said, 'Oh shit. I forgot to hang up the phone.'

There was a beat before you picked up the phone and asked, or rather demanded, 'Who is this?'

In the background a confused Adam said, almost defensively, 'I was leaving you a message.'

And then you said, 'Oh,' but you didn't hang up the phone because I could still hear you breathing, quick breaths like you'd just hit the pipe. Another moment passed before you said into the phone, obviously for my benefit, 'Hope you're having a good evening, Thompson. I certainly will.'

IT WAS DIFFICULT for me to process what you had just done since the Geico Waitress was handing off yet another glass of pink from an overflowing tray of

Cosmos that she claimed I'd ordered. The Gay Fiancé happily took them off my hands as my next message began to play automatically. It was the saved message from 'Do Not Answer' that I had banished to voicemail during the show.

The estranged voice said, 'Hi, Thom,' followed by a lengthy pause before he uncomfortably spat out, 'You're your father calling, Thom Thompson, Junior.' My heart dropped and I immediately wanted to hang up. The Gay Fiancé wanted me to hang up. The Geico Waitress really wanted me to hang up and settle my unsettling tab. But I didn't. Partly because I couldn't. Mostly because I was so unsettled by the fact that you had tricked Adam into sleeping with you and I desperately needed to be distracted by something, anything, and my stalker was obviously deranged enough to prove quite entertaining.

He cleared his throat and said, 'Not being part of your life has been one of my biggest regrets. What I did may seem horrible to you and the rest of the world, but only God will be the judge of that.' Then there was another chaotic, extremely awkward digitized gap before he continued, 'Anyhow, I'm pleased that I got to know you a little bit from watching *Big Brother*. Until I saw you all grown up on the show, I had trouble picturing you as anything but one of my two twin monsters crawling around the Nine-One-One.' Then there was another brief pause filled with a moist coughing attack, before he said, 'I'm dying and I don't have much time, Thom. It would be nice to reconnect before I go. I love you.'

ALTHOUGH I WAS STANDING beneath a heat-lamp at The Abbey, those three little words made me shiver. I'd never heard them before. Never once from Mommie Dearest. Well Adam had told me he loved me but he always said it during sex, on poppers, possibly when he was high, probably both. I never believed him. And it wasn't like I'd ever said those words either. Those words only count when you're compelled to say them first. Or possibly when you're sober.

Mostly I was shocked that my stalker mentioned you since I rarely talked about you to anybody, and I'd certainly never mentioned the fact that I had a brother on *Big Brother*, let alone a twin. It seemed prudent to avoid divulging personal information about our crazy family on a reality television show where I could be judged and have it used against me. Maybe it was because I felt ashamed that we had such a competitive, contentious relationship? Or possibly because I hated the inevitable probing questions about why I wasn't closer to my twin? But mostly it was because I loved the idea of not mentioning you and denying you any of my attention. For once in my life I could keep it all for myself. And yet somehow my stalker knew you existed. That, coupled with the fact that he knew about the Nine-One-One could only mean that he was telling the truth. That he was really our father. Daddy.

I began to dry heave behind the heat lamp until my eyes started to water. I couldn't remember the last time I'd eaten and my saliva was so thick I could hear the ping of my spittle as it dripped onto the heat-lamp's propane tank.

I WAS ALMOST AS DONE with The Abbey as I was with your bullshit, but for some reason I had this unexpected yet urgent need to tell you about Daddy even though I knew you wouldn't answer. I'd have to settle for nothing more than listening to your recorded voice on your outgoing message. But it didn't matter.

Partly because I was drunk. Mostly because I was still high. Regardless, I was overcome by this sobering faith that it didn't matter if I exposed my vulnerabilities to you anymore. I felt compelled to tell you that Daddy was alive. It felt like the right thing to do. My duty.

I gulped down my Cosmo and ordered another round from the Geico Waitress, partly because I needed the liquid courage, but mostly because I wanted to hear my own voice to make sure I wasn't slurring. The last thing I needed was for you to know I was drunk dialing you.

Your phone didn't even ring. And I never heard your voice because my call never went to voicemail. Instead I got cock-blocked by some telephonic bitch who informed me, 'The customer you are trying to reach is unavailable right now. Please try your call again later.' Although it felt like the omniscient disembodied voice was trying to save me from you, or possibly from my future embarrassment, I was pretty sure all it really meant was that you were delinquent on your phone bill.

After I hung up I habitually dialed Adam. When Adam didn't answer his cell I scrolled through my incoming call list and dialed the random (310) number he had called from earlier. The phone rang once before a perky woman answered and said, 'Four Seasons Hotel! How may I direct your call?'

I paused before stammering, 'I must have the wrong number,' then snapped my cell closed. I noticed a lingering stare from the Gay Fiancé who had finally moved on, but was now toasting me from across the crowded patio with a Cosmo that I had apparently paid for. I looked away from the desperate actor and desperately redialed my last incoming number, again, shaking my head as reality began to sink into my increasingly slushy head.

The Perky Receptionist answered, perkier than ever, 'Four Seasons Hotel! How may I direct your call?'

'Um,' my heart raced like it did back when I was broke and trying to score from an unsympathetic dealer. 'Adam Roth, please.' The layers of denial began to peel away as I wondered how much worse the day could get?

'Roth or Ross?' she asked as if the difference was negligible.

'R-O-T-H,' I spelled abruptly.

'I have no current hotel guests registered under that name. Could he be registered under another?'

I had no luck with your name and then there was an awkward pause before I gulped, 'How about Thom Thompson?'

'I'll put you through now,' said the Perky Receptionist. I became queasy with how far you were taking this *Parent Trap* twin-swap game, although your particular version was even trashier than the Lindsay Lohan remake.[20]

After a few rings, the phone was answered with a nonchalant, 'Hello?' but the voice on the other end of the line definitely did not belong to the registered guest.

'It's me.'

Adam said, 'Oh thank God. Where the hell are you?'

I wanted to tell him that he had just slept with an imposter, that he should get himself to the nearest free clinic and get an HIV test, that just because someone looks exactly like me, that he is not always going to be me. But I didn't say any of that because I had never mentioned you to Adam before and he didn't need another reason to think I was tweaked out of my skull. So I simply answered his question, 'I'm at The Abbey.'

---

[20] *The Parent Trap* is a 1998 remake of the 1961 family film of the same name, starring Lindsay Lohan in a dual role as twin daughters who are accidentally reunited after being separated at birth. The original, of course, is a classic, but the irony of Lindsay playing a Hayley Mills character can be written off as a guilty pleasure.

'The Abbey? Are you out of your mind? You need to get out of there before the news breaks. Don't you remember what we talked about? About the show?'

Of course I didn't remember what we talked about because I wasn't the one he had been talking to. I didn't know how to respond, didn't know how to explain, so I didn't say anything. That's when Adam told me to, 'Forget it. Stay there and do not leave. I'm coming to get you.'

Adam hung up and abandoned me to deal with the drunken designer jean parade at The Abbey. It wasn't long before the busy bar began to fade to black as if I was having an ocular migraine. Possibly an out-of-body experience. My field of vision began to close-in and darken until the drunken world around me dissolved slowly into nothing but a pinpoint. I was surrounded by darkness and began to feel like I was hovering over my boyfriend's hotel bed. Cheating on me. With you. With Rod Hard.

I PICTURED YOU and Adam enveloped by the emptiness of a luxurious Four Seasons suite on an upper floor with a desirable downtown view. The French doors to the balcony had been left open to expose the clear, neon sparkling skies of downtown Los Angeles. The lights were dimmed and raunchy gay porn was playing on the flat screen (obviously not yours as it would freak Adam out and blow your cover).

The room reeked of an accidentally spilled bottle of poppers and the nightstand overflowed with Viagra and random meth paraphernalia. The bed was unmade and the duvet had been carelessly thrown to the floor. The white, unfitted bottom sheet had been yanked, roughly, from all corners of the bed, exposing random patches of the plush, pillow-top mattress. On the sheet there was nothing remarkable besides an extremely discernible wet spot comprised of lube, cum and a puddle of poppers. The picture in my head was so realistic I felt like I was actually there.

THE GEICO WAITRESS returned around the same time as my consciousness and handed me yet another round of unnecessary cocktails that she, once again, assured me I'd ordered while I was on the phone. I reflexively stood up and put one cocktail down in order to collect the second, but was startled by the sudden dizziness that may or may not have been caused by too many Cosmos. I steadied myself by grabbing onto the waitress' shoulder, possibly her head, and somehow stumbled toward the bathroom without spilling a single drop. From either glass.

I wanted to lock myself in a stall, to hide away from everything, to shelter myself from anyone who might have the opportunity to see me get emotional, especially anyone with a camera. The stalls were as full as my bladder so I had the unfortunate choice of choosing between a middle urinal or queuing up behind a gaggle of greedy cokeheads. My bladder chose the urinal for me, mostly because I figured I'd draw less tabloid attention by exposing the leak above my waistline.

Ironically it was the leak below my belt which drew instant attention from some random Looky Loo at the next urinal who stared unapologetically at my crotch. One of the less appealing factors, yet daily occurrences of blending celebrity with a public toilet.

The Looky Loo said, 'Sorry to hear about your show,' never once looking away from my dick, even when I turned toward him and broke my unwritten law of never making eye contact at a urinal.

Confused, embarrassed, I began to panic but continued with the conversation so as not to appear like I was a hot mess. 'What are you talking about?'

'E! reported that it was the fall season's first casualty.'

'How is that possible? It doesn't even premiere until tomorrow night.'

He said, 'I have no idea,' then paused and grabbed his crotch for effect, 'Maybe you should ask, oh I don't know, *Rod Hard.*'

I looked down to watch my pee continue its counter-clockwise spiral down the urinal along with my career. Then there was an awkward silence, mostly because I knew he was telling the truth about the show. Rather than officially pull the plug, networks put shows on permanent hiatus so they won't have to deal with the disagreeable task of putting hundreds of people out of work.

If something unpleasant happens in Hollywood but it gets no media attention, does it really happen?

THE SHOCKING REALIZATION brought me right back to being blindsided when I was back-doored and voted off *Big Brother.* At least my housemates had the decency to look me in the face when they were canceling me.

There I was. At the urinal. In The Abbey. Blindsided once again. By the voicemail from my stalker who ended up being Daddy. By you shacking up at the Four Seasons with my boyfriend. By the unexpected news from the Looky Loo who was still staring at my goddamn dick. To add insult to injury the Looky Loo added, 'I saw a preview screener of the show and actually thought you were good.'

He actually said actually! And, actually, that was the straw that broke the camel's back. I asked as he flushed, 'You *actually* thought I was good? I'm so honored that the random pervert checking out my cock at the urinal *actually* thought I was good. Eyes on your own paper, asshole!'

'Don't get pissy with me, biatch. If you don't want people to look then you might consider not moonlighting in gay porn' he said, zipping up before quickly attempting to zip out of the bathroom.

'And don't forget to wash your pissy hands,' I snapped back as I buttoned up my Diesel's. After I got busted on national television for neglecting to visit the sink after visiting the *Big Brother* bathroom, I never, *ever* forgot to wash my hands après la toilette.

The Looky Loo turned on the faucet and glared at me in the mirror as he said, 'Actually, I was just being nice. Actually, I think your show sucks. Or should I say sucked?' He emphasized the past-tense while making an annoying tongue-in-cheek gesture to simulate a blowjob.

When I glanced back at my reflection I was horrified to notice tears streaming down my cheeks and immediately splashed water on my face for camouflage. Behind me one of the occupied stall doors swung open behind me and two Lady Boys walked out. The brunette rubbed his recently powdered nose as if he were Samantha's crack-whore cousin Serena on *Bewitched*.[21]

Embarrassed, I jumped at the opportunity to hide and cut in line ahead of the greedy cokeheads so nobody else would recognize me and watch my impending nervous

---

[21] *Bewitched* is a 1960s sitcom starring Elizabeth Montgomery as Samantha, a witch who marries an ordinary mortal man and tries to lead the life of a typical suburban housewife. Samantha's mischievous, lookalike cousin, Serena (also played by Elizabeth Montgomery) is the antithesis of Samantha, in most episodes sporting a beauty mark on her cheek, raven-black cropped hair and mod mini-skirts.

breakdown. Even though butting in line was a shitty, juvenile thing to do, the instantaneous mayhem it caused amongst the gays was nothing short of spectacular. Someone in the front of the line jumped up and we began to have a tug of war over the door as I attempted to lock it. Tears streamed down my face as I pushed my weight against the stall door to hold it closed, but slowly began to lose the battle. Eventually I let go and sat down on the toilet, attempting to cover my face from the aggressive cokehead. I was shocked when he pushed himself inside and proceeded to lock the stall door behind him. But I was even more shocked when I looked up and realized that he wasn't just anyone. He was you. You looked gaunt, wide-eyed, and somehow a bit more manic than you had that morning. You couldn't even focus on me as your pupils were darting back and forth like you were watching Wimbledon.

You postured yourself as if you were being mugged, possibly busted by the FBI, but it wasn't until I caught your jittering eye that I noticed the defeat behind your vacant look. It was only momentary, but I realized that you were just as lost as me. Possibly moreso. Or perhaps it had something to do with the fact that you were cracked out of your fucking skull.

That's when the Looky Loo yelled out, 'I hope that skinny little twink brought some Viagra, because Rock Hard doesn't quite live up to his name!'

'HOW DID YOU know I was here?' I wondered aloud.

'I know this because Tyler Durden knows this.'

I stifled the urge to smack you and your Chuck Palahniuk reference while you cackled through your smoker's hack. You paused before getting right to the point, 'Adam Roth doesn't mean anything to me,' as if that was supposed to make me feel better.

'So you slept with my boyfriend to spite me?'

'Once again, not everything is always about you, Thompson...'

'Happy birthday to you, too.'

'I don't have time for this shit! That's why I never call you back. You constantly need to analyze everything and I'm sick of it.' And then you said, verbatim, 'Which is exactly why I never call you back. You need to analyze everything, constantly, and I'm sick of it,' like you never said it the first time. You were obviously too twacked out to have a conversation.

We stood silently, crammed into the tiny bathroom stall as you plopped your glass pipe and lighter atop the back of the filthy porcelain toilet tank. All I cared about at that point was escaping the moment so I decided it was in my best interest to behave.

You pulled out a huge crystal which had an immediate silencing effect on me. It was so big that you had to break it into three pieces, crushing it on the back of the toilet tank with the bottom of the mini-Bic before one of the rocks could actually fit through the hole of your pipe. You lit up, took a big hit and held it deep in your lungs for a disturbingly long period of time before handing over the pipe. You said, 'Happy Birthday, little brother,' which always irked my liver since Mommie Dearest never bothered to inform us which one was older. Probably because she never knew. Most likely because she never cared.

I had never smoked meth before and was nervous, yet desperate for relief. Needless to say, my fear didn't last long. The pipe was handed back and forth, maybe a half dozen times, even though, after a few big hits, most of the crystal had liquefied. By the time you shoved the second crystal into the pipe, almost twice the size of the first, I already had a really nice high going. An exceptional tingly feeling from head to toe.

I took a hit and held it for what felt like thirty, maybe forty seconds. Only this time when I blew it out slowly, an intense, warm rush of euphoria washed over my entire body. I'd never felt anything like it before. Another exhilarating wave enveloped me with each breath I took. It was the purest high I'd ever experienced.

I was shocked, yet utterly defenseless when you placed the third crystal into the pipe and informed me, 'I still haven't got the right tweak.' I savored each and every subsequent puddle, between which my body swayed in harmony to the incredibly warm rushes while I rocked back and forth on the dirty, public toilet. It was, by far, the best feeling I'd ever had. From absolutely anything. Or anyone. Although I had always looked down upon addicts, suddenly I felt like I had just joined an exclusive club, along with you and Mother and her vast doll collection.[22] For the first time in practically ever, I felt like I belonged in our family. And it was blissful to finally feel so connected.

Previously my good highs on meth had come after snorting maybe five lines instead of the usual three, after which I'd become full of energy and felt like I could do anything. But that time was completely different. That time was euphoric. And for once I felt fortunate to be sharing a positive experience with you. Crystal was the one thing we had in common, the one thing we never argued about, the only thing we were good at as a team.

I began to talk aloud, softly, 'Ohmigod this feels so good. *Ohmigod.*' I swayed back and forth with each

---

[22] Valley of the Dolls is a novel by American writer Jacqueline Susann, published in 1966. The "dolls" within the title is a slang term for downers.

intensifying wave of pleasure and lost complete track of space and time in that filthy Abbey bathroom. Each time I tried to stand, the only thing I could bring myself to do was lean against the stall's wall, close my eyes and escape into the high's exquisite pleasure.

My eyes were closed when I began to worry if I'd ever be able to compose myself long enough to leave that bathroom stall. You kept grabbing at me, patting me on the stomach, assuring me everything would be okay. Kind of like a real big brother. And I believed you, mostly because, at that instant, everything was the most okay it had ever been.

THAT'S PROBABLY AROUND the time when you began to yank at my jeans. It wasn't until I finally opened my eyes and said rhetorically, 'What are you doing?' that I realized exactly what you were doing. You had unfastened my zipper and pulled down my Diesel jeans so quickly that my brand new 2Xist briefs got tangled in the folds, sliding down along with them. My forehead hit the toilet tank as you shoved my back down, spread my feet apart and pulled my bony hips toward you, toward Rod Hard. You reached around to cover my mouth so I couldn't breathe, let alone scream. You pulled me closer to my mirror image, my identical narcissist, and spat saliva into your hand before rubbing it on my cringing asshole.

The fact that you were barely hard didn't seem to bother you. It only made you push harder. A sinking feeling of déjà vu took over as I tried to stop you, tried to pull my pants back up, attempted to hold you back, pleaded with my eyes, but your ability to empathize, let alone reason, had obviously vaporized into white smoke several puddles ago.

I was physically trapped in the cold corner where the stall's steel divider met the filthy bathroom tiles as you, once again, attempted to thrust your semi-hard dick inside me. Even though we shared the same childhood and the same DNA, I found myself wondering who you were? You smelled so repulsive that I began to wonder when you had last bathed.

After a few failed attempts to rape me, I was finally able to push you off. You turned away from me in what I imagined to be the ultimate embarrassment, but little did I know you weren't done. You squeezed your face deep into the opposite corner of the stall and spread your legs wide so your loose skinny jeans could slide frictionlessly down your emaciated legs. With one hand you spread your butt cheeks wide apart, and with the other you pushed against the wall until your frail buttocks had me wedged me into the corner of the stall while you begged me to fuck you.

I screamed, 'What is wrong with you?!'

My only response was from an annoyingly familiar voice that lisped, 'Say Cheese!'

My dime-sized pupils retracted from the confusing strobe light that emanated from above. I looked up to find the Looky Loo, hovering above us, most likely standing on the toilet in the adjoining stall as he documented our ultimate sin in a flurry of extremely unflattering shots. You were oblivious. Or possibly didn't care. Your asshole continued to search for my dick like an insatiable truffle pig while your buttocks continued to pound against my pelvis. You muttered, 'Breed me,' as if you were Rod Hard. I tried to protect my eyes, to protect my identity by holding my hand up to the red-eye reduction stutter-flash, but had trouble focusing since I had become temporarily blinded by my personal paparazzo.

When you realized you weren't on a porn shoot, you attempted to pull your pants up and I was finally able to push you off. The Looky Loo laughed, maniacally, taking another round of embarrassing shots with his blinding red-eye reduction flash as I screamed something prosaic like, 'You fucking asshole!'

I jumped atop the toilet and tried to grab the camera from him but my reach caused me to slip and fall onto the filthy floor.

You were about as helpful as an anchor on the Titanic. I climbed over you and used my body weight as if I were attempting to right a capsized Catamaran. It took a while to pull up my jeans and regain balance so I could chase after the Looky Loo. He ran through the crowded outdoor patio, flailing his arms, screeching like a little girl. I tried to catch up but came to a grinding halt when I noticed that every patron was staring at me. Judging me. Possibly because my pants were hanging by my knees. But somehow, even after my Cosmopolitan crystal binge, I impressed myself when I shouted coherently into the crowd, 'He stole my camera!'

I assumed someone might help, but the next thing I knew, all of those same boys who couldn't get enough of me before, the same ones who, earlier, had practically lined up to hand me their head shots, the ones who had greedily accepted round after round of drinks on my tab, they all stood there, staring, judging my disheveled appearance while sipping from on their collective cocktail. It was like they all knew what had happened in that bathroom stall. They all knew about Rod Hard. They were disgusted. And thanks to my unfortunate jeans situation, I was practically immobilized. I had no choice but to let the Looky Loo escape with the photographic evidence while the Margarita-marinated mob continued to stare, point and eventually whisper.

I STOOD THERE, frozen amongst the gay chatter for God knows how long, until you nonchalantly emerged from that men's room, looking like nothing out of the ordinary had happened, appearing remarkably kempt for someone who had probably been fucked more times than he'd showered that week. And it was only Monday. Or technically the wee hours of Tuesday. For the first time in a very long time, everything seemed excessively clear to me.

I had to get out of The Abbey before Adam arrived. The idea of facing him in my current state was unbearable, to explain Rod Hard was unfathomable, but mostly I was motivated by my need to keep you away from him. After all those puddles in the bathroom, somehow it seemed far simpler to escape than try to explain that I wasn't the one dabbling in gay porn, that it was you, my twin brother who I'd never once mentioned, my doppelganger who'd gotten the show canceled. I had to get the hell out of Los Angeles, and unfortunately I had no choice but to take you with me.

I HANDED the cocktail waitress my Amex and asked to close my tab. She disappeared into the crowd when some random Armani Exchange poseur wearing a tank top (even though it was far too chilly) and a tight wool ski cap (even though it was far too warm) felt the urge to inform me that my zipper was down.

The fact that my zipper was down seemed so ridiculously absurd, so insanely inconsequential, so outrageously amusing that I began to howl at the overly underdressed hipster until he skulked away as if I were the ludicrous one. Of all the things I had to worry about: the fact that our dead father had actually been alive for the past two decades, the fact that our certifiably insane Mommie

Dearest had gone out of her way to fake his funeral, the fact that my twin brother's recent foray into gay porn had gotten my Adam's show canceled moments before it was supposed to premiere, the fact that you had tricked Adam into sleeping with you, and then, the fact that all of ridiculous mess had been topped off with an encore of attempted twincest, attempted rape in a public toilet—an unfortunate event which had been photographed, repeatedly. Yet on top of all this I needed to worry about plunging state of my zipper. It amused me so thoroughly that I willfully left it unzipped.

THE GEICO WAITRESS returned with the lovely parting gift of a disturbingly patriotic $1,776 bar tab (which luckily included the tip because I was in absolutely no mood for mathematics). I put my John Hancock on the historic bill and slithered toward the valet stand, squeezing past the burgeoning sidewalk sale of deeply discounted, drunken Abbey boys.

You followed me and habitually began chatting up the cracked-out Lady Boys from the men's room in such a way that I knew you wanted to hook up, wanted to ditch me, wanted to disappear. I couldn't tell which one you liked, most likely the lot of them, even though not one of them was remotely attractive. I kept an eye on you as I methodically searched through my pockets for the valet ticket, repeatedly, for several minutes, possibly twenty, until, sooner or later, I located it in my left hand.

I handed the ticket to the Parking Attendant with a folded twenty, hoping the bribe might speed the process of getting us away from that mess of messy boys. The whole time I tried eagerly to blend in to the crowd, to camouflage myself from a paparazzi helicopter while I waited for the

Valet to return. I wondered whether anybody could tell that I was flying higher than the helicopter, wondered whether they could tell I was pickled with Cosmos, wondered whether my two equally inebriated states had cancelled each other out to the point where it would be okay to drive?

I was so lost that I didn't notice the parking attendant, who was now standing directly in front of me, pointing to the fire engine red convertible as he said, 'I bring your car, no?' I chuckled, embarrassed, since I had been expecting my beige Budget rental which was so nondescript that it was prone to getting lost in Adam's driveway. I had literally forgotten about the Porsche. And until that moment I had also forgotten that Adam was on his way to get me.

I pushed through the ambivalent crowd, grabbed you away from the Lady Boys, and poured you into the passenger seat of the expensive roadster. It wasn't until I was sitting in the car that the Valet pointed out that I was still holding onto my Cosmo so I handed the half-finished glass to him as if he were moonlighting as a busboy. Luckily he didn't seem to mind.

Since the Valet had left the engine running, when I turned the key to make our getaway the Porsche made that upsetting, gear-grinding noise that sounded like Freddy Krueger sharpening his fingernail-knives against a blackboard. The Lady Boys on the sidewalk began to cackle, relentlessly, but I was no longer capable of registering embarrassment.

You asked, 'Where are we going?' And I had no idea how to respond.

My whole world had completely changed in the blink of an eye, kind of like the Porsche did when I finally located the convertible top button and allowed the darkness of another starless Los Angeles night envelop me like a black hole. I was mesmerized by the precision as the convertible gracefully reinvented itself, transforming from ragtop roadster into open-aired cabriolet. The electronic boot lifted, allowing the canvas top to fold away like an accordion until it ultimately vanished with no trace into the hidden compartment behind the tiny backseat which was much too cramped for anything beyond human torture. The experience was beyond compelling and, for a delectable instant, the world around me began to recede into a long forgotten memory.

Although I could barely recall what Daddy looked like, for those twenty-six seconds or so that it took to complete the convertible's transformation, I became flooded by memories from the day he brought home his brand new Porsche 911 Cabriolet. I remember being infatuated with watching him put the top up and down on his vintage Nine-One-One. The idea that a car could make such a drastic conversion with the push of a button seemed just as magical that day as it had almost two decades ago.

However, moments later, when every trace of the canvas roof had evaporated as if it never existed, so did my blissful twenty-six seconds of memory. Kind of like how our family ceased to exist after Mommie Dearest accidentally murdered Daddy. Kind of like how my career ceased to exist after you, or should I say Rod Hard, literally fucked me off the airwaves.

I WAS COMPLETELY preoccupied by my thoughtless thoughts until I heard Adam shout my name from the sidewalk. 'I told you to wait for me!' We both turned and when I recognized his confusion over my body double riding shotgun, I had no choice but to pop the clutch and make it all go away.

The sports car roared north as I merged onto Robertson, whisking me and my far-too-conscious state far away from The Abbey, but it wasn't long before the street lit up as if they were shooting day-for-night. I looked up at the helicopter, squinting, shading my overly-dilated pupils from the paparazzo's blinding klieg light. I wondered if they were they looking for Rod Hard? Or possibly the LAPD was? I didn't wait around to find out.

I slammed the gas pedal to the floor and the Porsche easily accelerated to fifty miles per hour before I remembered to shift into second gear. I ran the red light on Santa Monica, partly because I needed to escape any further exposure from Big Brother's floating spotlight, but mostly because the thought of accidentally glancing into my rearview mirror and catching Adam's eye while waiting for the light to change was completely unbearable.

I needed distance from the past, no matter how recent. I needed to escape the present with reckless abandon and lunge into the future with a turbo charged engine. I felt anxious as I whizzed past the ubiquitous 'Welcome to Beverly Hills' sign. Up until that point, I'd actually found the illuminated moniker comforting, but all of a sudden the ridiculously false serenity of the moneyed utopia felt like it was mocking me. Beverly Hills was nothing more than a tropical, palm-tree'd version of the taunting New England town we grew up in. A painful yet luxurious reminder of the past I'd worked so hard to escape, to forget. The sense of residential déjà vu became even more stifling after a series of abrupt, random turns, all vain attempts to escape any possible confrontation with Adam.

We whizzed past stately mansions which seemed to be growing—literally bulging from their property lines as if they'd been abusing steroids imported from Todd Tramp's personal training gym in WeHo.

The Porsche flew past McMansions like a cannonball on the aptly named Cañon Drive as we soared toward Sunset. I ignored the pesky stop signs, because much like my relentless thoughts, it had become impossible for me to stop. It wasn't long before I encountered a fork in the road and was forced to make a decision. But it wasn't just any fork. I had stumbled upon Malfunction Junction, that dodgy intersection of Cañon, Beverly and Lomitas where each road reached out in different directions, like the arms of a starfish, offering far too many choices for my tweak, and ultimately inciting panic. Choosing a direction proved more challenging than picking a dish from the bible-sized menu at Mel's Drive-In on the Strip. Unable to stop driving in circles, my indecision culminated into an endless series of squealing donuts, smack in the middle of the massive intersection. As the Porsche spun in actual circles, my mind was caught in the psychological equivalent while I examined the pros and cons of each direction of escape.

It wasn't long before I found myself confessing to you, 'Daddy isn't dead. Not yet anyway.'

'What the fuck are you talking about?'

'My stalker left a voicemail during the show. He said some things that made me realize he isn't full of shit. That he's really Daddy. He also told me he was dying'

Without saying a word you grabbed my cell from the center console, scrolled through my call log and placed a call to Daddy. I quickly did the time-zone math and tried to grab the phone back, 'What are you doing? It's five-thirty in the morning there!' By the time I pulled the car to the side of the road it was too late.

You were slouched in the bucket seat with your dirty shoes on my brand new dashboard as you said 'Is this Thompson Thompson, Jr.?' There was a long beat before you identified yourself, 'This is your other son, the one you didn't bother to name yourself after, the one you didn't bother to tell that you were alive.' There was a disturbingly long pause before you raised your voice, 'Of course this is Timothy! Did you forget that you had twins?' And with that your bad temper stomped your heel into the stereo.

'What the fuck are you doing?' I screamed as the music disappeared along with my cell which you threw into someone's yard.

I immediately ran over to retrieve it from the newly cut grass while you continued to pout in the car. 'Hello?' I asked, hoping that Daddy hadn't hung up, 'Daddy? This is Thom. I'm really sorry. Tim isn't quite himself right now.'

There was a long pause before Daddy said tentatively, 'Thom, is everything okay?'

'More or less,' I lied.

'Timothy is dead.'

'What are you talking about? He's right here.'

You said, 'I don't want to talk to him.'

'Timothy died in The Accident.'

'I don't understand. We thought you were the one who died in The Accident.'

There was a long pause before I could hear a woman's voice ask Daddy in the background, 'Who are you talking to at this hour?'

Then Daddy said, 'Thom, I have brain cancer and I can't handle this kind of stress right now.' Then he hung up. And just like that, I finally decided where I wanted to go. Or needed to.

AT FIRST YOU PROTESTED, 'Why would I want to reunite with a man who abandoned us to be raised by a woman who should have abandoned us?!'

'Because he's our father. And he has brain cancer. It might be our last chance to meet him.'

'Does he have any money? Do you think he'll put us in his will?'

If nothing else you were predictable when it came to money and financing your delusions. 'How the hell should I know? Until an hour ago I assumed he was an insane fan. Besides, what does it matter? He's our father. Isn't that enough?'

'I can't leave L.A. There's a porn shoot in the Valley tomorrow morning. My first featured role.'

'It's 2:30am and you smoked an entire baggie of crystal. You won't even be able to get it up!'

'I'm just bottoming. Besides it's not like you can leave. What about your show?'

I'd never seen you more pleased than when I informed you, 'The show got canceled because they thought I was Rod Hard.' After that you didn't seem to care much about your porn shoot or where we went.

THERE WAS ONE LAST THING I wanted to do before leaving L.A. It wasn't long before we were sailing back down Sunset Boulevard, back toward West Hollywood, back toward the billboard.

The open road slowed to a cruising crawl by the time I crossed back over Doheny onto the western edge of the Sunset Strip. It wasn't long before I was being teased by Talesai, the restaurant I attempted to ignore as we passed by the spot where Adam Roth had initially offered me the part on *Wall Street Widows* over gallons of Mai Tais. Traffic crawled past the Hustler store and I found myself rubbernecking the crowd of tourists gathered on the sidewalk in front of the Viper Room, seemingly holding yet another impromptu River Phoenix memorial. Then, just as we crept past San Vicente, some drunken *Big Brother* fan screamed out my name from the sidewalk, 'Thom!' Instinctively you waved back as if you were still pretending to be me.

The nightclub traffic ground to a halt as quickly as I was grinding the enamel from my teeth. It didn't matter much, because in the distance I was transfixed by the fifty foot advertisement of Neil Patrick Harris and me, perched high above the Sunset Strip, urging motorists to watch 'The Fall's most anticipated new comedy, *Wall Street Widows!* Tuesdays at 9:30!' However the message had definitely lost any sense of urgency since someone had spray painted a graffiti cock, going into my mouth.

Traffic kept us a Hollywood hostage, forcing me to bear witness to my public blowjob until I couldn't bear to look at myself for one more millisecond. Although I was totally stuck in gridlocked traffic, I cranked the steering wheel until the power steering began to whine. Then I popped the clutch so fast that the Porsche jerked up onto the sidewalk. My erratic driving jolted an unsuspecting pedestrian in front of Book Soup to the point where she jumped into a bush for safety. I continued to drive down the sidewalk until I cleared the traffic, then raced down Holloway, away from the Sunset Strip, away from the City of Angels, away from my own personal 'Disappear Here'[23] billboard as fast as I possibly could. I needed to disappear on my own terms before I became completely lost beneath the Hollywood graffiti and ultimately forgotten, just like Daddy.

---

[23] 'Disappear Here' is an ominous billboard that Clay drives by repeatedly in *Less Than Zero*, most likely to hit us over the head with clever symbolism, rather than simply referencing it.

AT THAT VERY MOMENT I knew I needed to find out what exactly happened all those years ago, find out why Daddy disappeared from our lives, why Mommie Dearest had faked his funeral. I needed to find him, to meet him before it was too late and ask him why? I thought of nothing else as I sped down La Cienega.

It was an unusually warm desert night and I was wide awake. I thought going for a nice long drive in the open air would do us both some good so I plugged in our old Hell's Kitchen zip code into the Porsche's GPS as I merged onto the eastbound lanes of the 10 Freeway. The GPS informed me that it would take approximately one-day-and-seventeen hours to drive the two-thousand-seven-hundred-ninety-six miles to New York. I was so deeply lost in the mathematics of our impending transcontinental road trip that I practically sideswiped an ominous Buick Skyhawk that was spray-painted matte-black and had tinted windows and government issued plates. That's when my inner Clay remembered the well documented fact, 'People are afraid to merge on freeways in Los Angeles.'[24]

---

[24] The opening line of Bret Easton Ellis' *Less Than Zero* whose narrator Clay returns to his hometown of Los Angeles, California for winter break during the early 1980s and embarks on a series of drug-fueled nights of partying, during which he picks up various men and women for one-night-stands. Sound familiar?

7

YOU ARE SITTING in the cramped backseat of your new Porsche staring at this giant, unsettling billboard of yourself. Your graffitied image, our graffitied image, stares back, judgmentally, from high above the Sunset Strip. The top is down, the sun is warm and the thick Santa Ana winds swirl around you—stifle you—while an old Thompson Twins song plays on the stereo. 'You told me you loved me, so I don't understand, why promises are snapped in two, words are made to bend?' You are more than a bit surprised to find Mommie behind the wheel since you can't recall the last time she had left the house, let alone drove. She looks much younger and almost pretty. She turns toward you, lip-syncing in perfect time to the chorus, 'Lies, lies, lies, ye-ah! Lies, lies, lies, ye-ah!' It is more than a bit troubling since Mommie is crying. You ask her if everything is okay since black mascara tears are streaming down her face. She ignores you and looks back to the road. Mommie makes a harsh left, then pounds the gas pedal just before Sunset-Gower studios. The car races north across Hollywood Boulevard, beneath the 101 freeway overpass, and then speeds toward the hills. You look up to the sky but are confused since the convertible top has somehow converted into a sunroof. In fact, you realize that the Porsche has morphed into another car entirely—specifically your mother's old Audi 5000. You muster up enough courage to ask Mommie, 'Where are you taking me?' but she is weeping and can't answer. Won't answer. She turns up the stereo, probably to drown out your incessant line of questioning while she continues to lip-sync, 'Do I have to catch you out to know what's on your mind?' Mommie makes a right onto Franklin followed by a quick left into Beechwood Canyon. She is driving much too fast, barely able to see the road through her bleeding mascara as she delves deeper into the hills, roaring past Madonna's ostentatiously striped, Spanish-style house as she barrels north toward Mulholland.

You stare out the window to calm your nerves and are surprised to recognize old Victorians with big porches and Colonial style houses from back east. Houses from your childhood. From Old Greenwich. Somehow Mulholland has blended into Sound Beach Avenue as Mommie zooms past Binney Park and then through the quaint little village, past Garden Catering and Curry's where you learned the meaning of a five-finger discount. She is driving fast. Disturbingly fast. Your anxiety heightens as Mommie's driving becomes increasingly erratic. She disregards stop lights and slaloms around little landscaped traffic circles which have been deliberately placed in the sleepy town to deter speeding. Her light blue Audi continues to accelerate as it turns down Lockwood, then, like a homing pigeon, it squeals onto Tomac, racing toward your familiar driveway. 'Cleopatra died for Egypt, what a waste of time.' Your heart pounds with déjà vu as Mommie plows down the white pebbled driveway of the historic white Sea Captain's home you grew up in. But the house is in perfect condition—nothing at all like the decrepit house you remember, the house the Preps at the bus stop gleefully mocked as Gay Gardens. The paint is not chipping and the grounds are so well manicured they are equally unrecognizable. You barely remember the boxy Widow's Walk, proudly protruding from the flat roof since long ago it had been hit by lightning and burned through the ceiling, making the entire third floor of the house uninhabitable by the time you entered Middle School. White driveway pebbles crunch beneath the Audi's alloy wheels as the car approaches the surprisingly stately home. It actually reminds you of old photographs you found hanging in the Innis Arden Clubhouse that time when you broke-in to steal liquor from the wood paneled bar. The Audi's tires screech even louder than you, violently spitting pebbles as they attempt to achieve traction. Mommie is driving much too fast toward the detached garage which has several enormous black crows, possibly ravens, perched ominously atop the ornate weather vane on the roof. You continue to scream, begging Mommie to slow down. To stop. To reconsider. But she is too busy singing, practically yelling, 'White ones and red ones, and some you can't disguise! Twisted truth in half the news! Can't hide it in your eyes!

Lies, lies, lies, ye-ah!' Mommie is much too focused on her target to pay attention to your plea. Daddy stands there, visibly confused by the speed of his wife's approaching Audi as he waters plants in the long since dried-up, yet once lavishly landscaped backyard. You attempt to scream, to warn Daddy since you already know what is going to happen, but your voice doesn't work. No words, not even a whisper will emanate from your eager mouth. A moment later, when the song reaches its crescendo, you know what is about to happen. There is no turning back, 'You say you'll try harder, but I think it's just too late! Well, the car is revving in the drive, and I'm not the sort to wait!' Everything switches into slow motion, seemingly for no other reason than to prolong the painful anticipation of impact. After a few endless moments the expression on Daddy's face turns from confusion to terror. He races across the lawn, up the hill, toward the swimming pool, away from the approaching Audi which follows him like a guided missile. Incredulous, Daddy takes one last look at the woman he married, for better or worse, before she runs him over with her brand new car. Fully clothed in a pin striped, double breasted Brooks Brothers suit, Daddy attempts to dive into the pool, but the Audi is too fast. The impact happens mid-air. The windshield shatters as it swallows Daddy's shoulder. The engine redlines as the car briefly becomes airborne, and then quickly sinks into the deep end of the expansive, black-bottomed swimming pool. 'The bigger, the better, some nicked from old Saigon. Collected from around the world, love lies on and on and on and on and on...' You panic as water seeps through the open sunroof, quickly flooding the Audi's interior. Somehow the radio continues to play even though the power windows have shorted out. Even if you were stronger than the water pressure that holds your door tightly in place, opening it proves impossible since all the doors are jammed against either side of the swimming pool's retaining wall. Your pulse throbs inside your oxygen starved brain until your lungs became completely overwhelmed. 'Lies, lies, lies, ye-ah! They're gonna get you! Lies, lies, lies, ye-ah! They won't forget you!' You can't take the pressure in your lungs or the pounding in your head anymore so you reluctantly give in to the involuntary reflex and you…

…gasped as my panicked lungs expected to fill with chlorinated water but surprisingly awakened to the pungent new car scent. Terrified, I opened my eyes which thankfully pulled me out of the groggy state of my recurring nightmare. I awoke to find myself in a fetal position, crammed into what Porsche designers drolly refer to as a backseat. I remember crawling back there to try and get some sleep when we were driving through Pittsburgh, but waking up in Manhattan was unnerving. I felt like Robert Downey, Jr. waking up in a place he never remembered falling asleep in. It wouldn't have surprised me had I woken up in a stranger's bed, in the Malibu Colony. In fact I would have much preferred it, but my whereabouts were the least of my concerns since everything located between my charred lips and my bulging blisters hurt in a way that, until that point in time, had been unimaginable. Like every other time I emerged from hibernation after a binge during the past year, I swore to myself that I was done with meth. That I'd never do it again. And yet in the same breath I'd be snorting another bump, 'Just to get me through the morning,' I'd tell myself repeatedly.

The incessant throbbing in my head was exacerbated by erratic pounding on the windshield. The excruciating ratio of noise to pain did nothing but stimulate my need to sleep, to disappear. My tactic of non-response worked for a bit as the knocking subsided momentarily, leaving me in the excruciating solitude of honking taxis, screaming pedestrians and wailing sirens that made up the ridiculously shrill, hangover-unfriendly mosaic that could only be described as Manhattan's morning rush hour.

The non-stop cross country drive felt like an intense thirty-nine hour time-lapse video without a soundtrack since you had kicked the shit out of the radio. We did a shitload of crystal and sought relief amongst horny truckers and overly caffeinated drinks. Besides that, we never stopped. Not even to eat. I remember you tried to talk me into one last bump somewhere between Toledo and Cleveland, and I remember telling you that if I kept burning the nostrils at both ends then my septum would wear out faster than a goddamn candle. So

Instead I hit the pipe even though the shadow people had really started to upset me. I first started noticing them when we were driving through the high wheat plains in remote Kansas. It was totally Holcomb. Very *In Cold Blood*.[25] Once I began to see them—those terrifying figments of people with sinister motives and fluid movements—I saw them everywhere. In the rearview mirror, standing at the edge of a cornfield, leaping across a cement barricade, jumping at me from passing tractor trailers, grabbing at me through filthy restroom windows. Luckily with enough concentration I could usually will them to disappear. Usually.

I WAS JOLTED awake again when the car literally began to take flight as if it were Greased Lightning during the end credits of *Grease*. Unlike Olivia Newton John, I already knew it was not going to be a happy ending for me.[26]

---

[25] *In Cold Blood* is a non-fiction novel by Truman Capote detailing the brutal murders of Herbert Clutter, a successful farmer from Holcomb, Kansas, his wife, and two of their four children. It's a tad bit heavier than *Breakfast at Tiffany's*.
[26] "This car could be systematic. Hydromatic. Ultramatic. Why, it could be

I was more despondent than elated, but had no choice but to lift my impossibly heavy eyelids in an attempt to peer out the windshield, which was obstructed by a tacky silver sunshade I didn't remember purchasing. The side and rear windows were also covered. Wallpapered, actually, with aluminum foil. Obviously due to one of your increasingly paranoid delusions.

When I removed the sunshade I realized that it was only the front hood of the Porsche that had taken flight, with the help of a friendly tow truck and a less-than-friendly tow truck driver. The man was less-than-nonplussed to find a hostage inside his soon-to-be impounded car. He screamed, 'Alternate side parking! Alternate side parking!' which at the time seemed non-sensical.

Eventually, I gathered enough energy to overcome my gravity deficiency and pushed the passenger seat forward. Unfortunately the act of movement also released a troubling stench that emanated somewhere deep from within the crotch of my Diesel jeans. I momentarily debated allowing myself to get towed away with the car, but ultimately found enough momentum to swing open the passenger door. An inch. The Reynolds Wrap fell to the street and revealed a sadistically bright orange parking violation sticker that had been pasted to the window by an angry Meter Maid. Somehow I muttered the words, 'It's okay, I'll move it,' with a voice that was shakier than my hands. My vocal cords were so fried that I didn't recognize the raspy voice as my own. I sounded more like you.

My teeth felt like a sweet old granny had knitted them a wool sweater and I was completely unprepared for the consequences of dialog. Yet there I was, disengaged in a one-way screaming match with a high pitched, Chihuahua-

---

Greased Lightning!" If you haven't seen the movie musical *Grease* about a bunch of thirty-year-olds playing high school students, shame on you.

sized tow truck driver who sounded like Rosie Perez's brother yapping at me in a language that may or may not have been Newyorican hybrid of Spanglish.

Since the front of the car had already been lifted by the tow truck, Rosie Perez's Brother held open the gravity-challenged door, enabling me to stumble onto the sidewalk. His indecipherable sentences were peppered with extremely decipherable words like, 'homeless,' 'smelly' and 'stolen.'

Until I stubbed my toe on the pavement I had no idea that I was both barefoot and shirtless. Instinctively I reached into my back pocket so I could throw money at the elevating situation, but, just like you, my wallet was also missing.

I searched for it everywhere, frantically, paranoid that I had been robbed. As I sifted through the contents of the glove compartment I ended up stumbling upon some disconcerting Budget paperwork and realized that Adam had not actually bought me the Porsche. He rented it. For a week. And now it was being towed away. Three thousand miles away from the Beverly Hills Budget Rental Car's luxury division. But I was feeling so terrible that I only cared about getting past the moment, even if it meant giving the ninety thousand dollar car away.

I'M NOT SURE how long I stood there, weighing my dwindling options as I watched the rented Porsche get towed down 17th Street. People were looking at me. Staring. Some pointed. Most whispered. It wasn't long before I noticed a brand new W Hotel in Union Square across the street and although I was mortified by my appearance, my odor, my lack of money, my lack of clothing, and my recent lack of transportation, I decided to go inside the hotel and ask for help. Beg for it. There was nothing to lose since I literally had nothing.

The hotel was imposing in such a way that I began to wonder if their toilet paper might be made of Egyptian cotton with a 600-thread count. I waited in line for the concierge, with no shirt, no shoes, and no hope for service. I ignored stares and began to concoct a story about being mugged, raped and possibly murdered. I'd say anything that would get the man to patch me through to American Express, wondering if I had paid my bill, hoping that you hadn't exhausted my available credit, praying that Amex would authorize payment for a room, if for no other reason for me to take a four hundred dollar shower.

The concierge was still on the phone when he called out my name, 'Mr. Thompson.' He sounded unnerved, like he knew me. Like he was having déjà vu and we'd already been through this embarrassing situation once before. His guard was up in a way that I knew he didn't recognize me from *Big Brother.* 'What can I help you with this morning?'

'Um,' I stammered, 'I feel like a complete idiot, but I seem to have been mugged and was wondering if you could patch me through to American Express.'

'I'm so sorry about that,' he feigned. 'Usually they can have a new card delivered the very next day. Will you need a replacement room key, too?'

I stared at the concierge, dumbfounded, until he actually had to repeat his question, which gave me just enough time to process the fact that you had checked into a room, using my wallet, my credit cards, and were pretending to be me, again. I answered nonchalantly, 'That'd be great. And don't worry about calling Amex. I can do that myself. From my room.'

'No worries,' he said as he wrote something down on a piece of paper. A clandestine note he placed in my hand as if he were slipping me his number, or attempting to warn me about something. Possibly someone. Probably you.

It felt like a trap and I was scared to look at it until he reminded me, 'That's the number for American Express,' which, of course, I had long since forgotten about since I no longer needed to call Amex. I was obviously still tweaking and not gotten enough sleep after the longest cross-country binge I'd ever been on.

Unfortunately I had absolutely no idea which room you were in so I had no choice but to embarrass myself further, 'Could you remind me of my room number again?'

The Concierge gave me a once over before dipping back into his computer screen. As he typed my name my paranoia heightened and I worried whether he was really a concierge at all. His suit was as nondescript as a General Motors full-sized, beige sedan. It screamed government employee. For chrissakes it was practically a $99 Men's Warehouse special. Whatever the unfortunate brand, it definitely did not belong in an upscale hotel like the W. A suit like his belonged in a Federal Building. I tried to sneak a look at his shoes for verification, but they were hidden from view behind his marble pedestal.

I braced myself for the inevitable, to be stopped, caught, arrested, and put in jail for something you had done. Something terrible. So when he told me the room number and handed me the key card I had no choice but to exhale a hefty sigh. I immediately went to my room. Your room. Our room.

I LET A FEW crowded elevators pass in order to wait for a private one. I was embarrassed by my unfortunate lack of wardrobe, by my emaciated body, but it seemed preferable to stand there, barefoot and bare-chested, than share a crowded elevator with curious strangers with a keen sense of smell.

Eventually I was whisked up to the twentieth floor with such speed that my knees felt weak as if I might swoon. However, my light-headed, woozy feeling was nothing compared to the way I felt when I unlocked the door to the penthouse suite you had thoughtfully booked with my rapidly dwindling credit. You even went as far to welcome me with a 'Do Not Disturb' sign hanging from my doorknob, like a noose.

THE BEDROOM DOOR inside the suite was closed so I decided to take a shower before confronting you. Remember how Daddy used to plug his nose and say, 'My first *odor* of business is to get you boys a bath!' I hadn't thought about him for years and suddenly I was being flooded with long lost memories.

When I turned toward the bathroom door I immediately noticed random clothing strewn around the bedroom. Pants on the floor. My filthy sneakers next to the couch. An expensive suit draped carefully over the back of the desk chair. Several designer tank tops. Even my favorite 'Fuck Me I'm Famous' t-shirt. My missing wallet. Most of the credit cards were intact, along with my ATM so it wasn't completely tragic that you'd spent all the cash.

The bathroom was beyond luxurious and I felt horny just standing there. I briefly considered taking a romantic bath by myself, but ultimately determined that sitting in a stagnant tub of my own filth would inevitably prove to be counter-productive.

Before hopping into the steaming shower I peeled off my pungent underwear and threw it into the trash. I needed to be clean. To cleanse myself. I scrubbed filth from my body until the little hotel bar of soap actually disappeared into my twitching hand, much in the same way that I happily disappeared under the fire hose-like stream of hot water. I hibernated for what felt like an entire television season. When the hot water began to cool I dried off and wiped down the foggy mirror to stare at my disturbing nakedness. My bony body was shocking. I was beginning to look more like you than me.

I STOLE A PAIR of Calvin Klein underwear that I found on the floor of the suite's living room and had one leg back into my Diesel jeans when a huge, previously unnoticed and currently unattended bag of crystal on the coffee table demanded my attention. The slight vapors from an recently abandoned pipe coaxed me, seduced me to give up on my ridiculous, yet almost daily vow to stop using. I, of course, immediately gave in to the non-existent pressure and took a quick hit. Then another incremental one. Much deeper. I needed to be sufficiently high to prepare myself for you and whatever else I'd find on the other side of the bedroom door. I considered smoking the whole stash, but there was too much, even for me.

It wasn't long before my attention deficit gravitated toward the south facing windows to inspect an ominous plume of mysterious white smoke that poured from Lower Manhattan. The cloud was so thick and voluminous that it literally blocked the World Trade Center in its entirety. My immediate response was to turn on the news but I became distracted by an anxious knock at the door. I wondered what kind of ridiculously expensive, outrageously cliché item you had ordered from room service. Dom Perignon? Beluga Caviar on toast points? A Brazilian Bellboy? But as the knocking got louder, more urgent, very official, I began to worry that the Men's Warehouse concierge had caught on to me. Or even worse, had caught on to you.

I stood there, panicked, until I heard the bedroom door open. I braced myself your tirade, but when you passed by on the way to answer the door I realized that you weren't you at all. Instead some strange naked Latino man with a sunken face and a raging, uncut hard-on emerged from the bedroom and eagerly raced over to the peep hole like a city kid without a chimney who was waiting for Santa Claus.

It was odd that the Latino didn't notice me, though he was obviously high as a kite. That's when I heard your raspy voice yell from the bedroom, 'Is he hot? Send him away if he's not hot!'

'He's a'ight. Another Asian.' Then he mumbled, 'Fuckin' Craigslist orgies.'

'Don't let him in unless he's got Viagra!' you hollered back, obnoxiously. 'Too much crystal dick already. Besides we don't need another bottom!' But I could tell the Latino was a bottom feeder by the way he opened the door. Some twink entered. Actually he looked more like a tween who had skipped his pre-algebra class so he could join in on your PnP festivities.[27] The Latino Bottom Feeder actually nodded to me, nonchalantly, then told the Twinky Asian to help himself to some Tina in the living room and to get his hot ass into the bedroom when he was feeling good and ready.

The kid introduced himself and I prayed that he wouldn't recognize me, 'I can't believe how long it took me to get here. The F train is all fucked up this morning.' I forced a weak smile until he asked, 'You on your way in or out?' as if we were both auditioning for the featured role of 'Crackhead.'

---

[27] PnP is gay slang for Party n' Play, which typically involves Crystal Meth (Party) & Sex (Play).

I ignored his question mostly because I became completely fixated as he crushed a nice fat crystal into a long fat line. I began to salivate like Pavlov's dogs when the Twinky Asian grabbed a burnt glass cylinder from the coffee table and methodically ran it over a handy handheld blowtorch until it began to glow. He had the focus of a Venetian glassblower with centuries of family experience.

I became mesmerized watching him silently heat the glass cylinder with the lighter, practically burning off his fingerprints during the seductive process. The pipe was almost molten when he hovered above the lengthy rail and snorted. The crystals vaporized inside the glass straw milliseconds before reaching his nostrils, and I watched his eyes euphorically roll back into his head before he dropped down onto the carpet and let the wave take over.

Unfortunately I was already much too high to experiment with hot-rails but I watched the Twinky Asian with envy until he got back up on his feet and offered me his burnt glass cylinder, 'Care for a hot-rail?' I shrugged and without further ado, he disappeared down the hall into a chorus of (mostly) masculine moans.

Instinctively I shoved the baggie, glass cylinder and blow torch into my pocket figuring it was collateral since you had obviously rented the room with my credit card, used my drugs and stole my cash, not to mention my identity. But as soon as I walked into that room I wished I had smoked the entire baggie, plastic and all, because I was completely unprepared for what I found.

THERE WERE AT LEAST six guys, maybe more. It was hard to count as the bed was just a mass of penises, sweaty limbs and cum-stained sheets. Although it was obviously gender-biased, the room was so racially, culturally and socially diverse that it felt like a gay Benetton advertisement. I couldn't even locate the little Asian Twink amongst the sea of erections. Gay porn starring Rod Hard was playing on the plasma TV and some big bear with a hairy back and a tattooed sleeve lisped orders to everyone while filming the whole thing from a tripod in a dark corner as if he were a slightly more masculine Chi Chi LaRue.[28]

You were facing away, getting fucked doggie style by the Latino Bottom Feeder who couldn't have been more focused on your ass had he been a proctologist. Meanwhile some ginger Prep with shockingly red pubes was shoving his freckled dick in your face, slapping you on the cheek with it, ordering you to 'Choke on that.' You, however, were much too preoccupied holding the belt strap tautly with your teeth, multi-tasking as you attempted to find a vein. After the Latino Bottom Feeder shot you up with God knows what, you gladly rewarded the Hairy Prep's patience with your voracious mouth, swallowing him whole without the slightest indication of a gag reflex. Someone's hand, perhaps the black body builder with dreads, or possibly it was the bald guy with the big Buddha belly, honestly it didn't matter which, but one of them eagerly grabbed your dirty syringe and eagerly recycled the needle, Rod Hard's needle, deep into his track ridden forearm.

With two Viagra'd dicks pounding you from either end (not to mention a third one in the hand you weren't using to support yourself), you finally caught my eye in the oversized mirror hanging over the desk. You said nothing, just kept sucking on the Ginger Prep's freckled dick while you stared through me. We looked at each other for a beat, until your eyes began to dart around the room like a cat in

---

[28] Larry David Paciotti is a highly successful American film director of gay, bisexual and straight pornography, but the bitch is best known for her drag persona, Chi Chi LaRue.

heat. You were so high I couldn't tell where your pupils ended and your iris began, but your eyes were much too busy to focus on anything in particular. Perhaps they couldn't. For the first time in a very long time I felt like I was seeing you clearly, witnessing who you truly were, who you had become, Rod Hard, and where the two of you were headed. I was terrified. When our eyes caught in the mirror again, like Alice through her looking glass, you asked, 'Care to join our ménage-a-six? Perhaps this time you'll actually finish what we started?'

I lost it, 'Do you know how fucked up, how revolting, how disgusting, how morally reprehensible the idea of having sex with my twin brother is?! I feel nauseous just thinking about what happened at The Abbey!'

That's when the Ginger Prep put his dick back in your mouth and said, 'Dude, you're really shackling my buzz.'

I LITERALLY RAN out of the hotel and continued running down the street and into the park but the pedestrian gridlock in Union Square felt post-apocalyptic. I was immediately overwhelmed by a familiar odor. It was saccharine, almost toxic, like burning plastic, and like most everything else, triggered my sense-memory into a longing for crystal meth vapors. The scent, however, was the only thing that was the least bit comforting as it felt like I had stumbled into a pandemic. Something was obviously very wrong as every somber face on the street was obscured by a white painter's mask.

The masked faces, however, were not nearly as disturbing as the Xeroxed ones which were plastered upon every available surface in Union Square. The flyers pled silently to help find missing loved ones, and their photos, obviously taken during happier times, seemed disturbingly naïve compared to the masked faces surrounding me, many of whom were crying as they scanned the wall beside me.

I was struck by the qualitative and quantitative differences between the missing person's 'Have you seen me?' flyers. Some were barely recognizable black and white photocopies with nothing but a name and phone number. Others were part of elaborate campaigns, practically wallpapering the park with colorful Kodak collages, expertly produced to help locate them. However the one thing all those poor people had in common, those ghosts that littered the park like battlefield casualties, was that they all worked in the World Trade Center.

I looked up into the southern sky but no matter where I stood I could not find the Twin Towers in the skyline. It was absurd. I ran south through the park, toward University, to a point where I knew I would have an unobstructed view of them—but they weren't there. They had been replaced by an enormous, billowing white cloud of smoke that that was headed for Brooklyn. Although it was beyond comprehension, the World Trade Center was absolutely, without a doubt, gone.

The fact that two planes could coincidentally collide into the iconic buildings was truly unbelievable, but the fact that I was so tweaked out of my skull that I hadn't been aware it even happened was what even moreso.

INCOMPREHENSIBLE feelings that had been simmering deep beneath the surface began to boil over. I felt like I was being microwaved on high, being radiated from the inside out. I was completely ambivalent. I didn't know what to feel.

I crumbled onto a park bench, practically onto the laps of random strangers who awkwardly hopped onto another bench as I commanded myself to feel something.

LONG BEFORE our despondent Mommie Dearest could arrange Daddy's fake funeral, I remember being extremely confused about why he had disappeared. So confused that I decided to go and find him. Before I ran away I packed some clothes into a brown paper Food Mart shopping bag along with Figment, the stuffed animal that Daddy had given me. Although I remembered to pack clothes, unfortunately I had forgotten to wear any. I think it was Mrs. Bourne who found me crossing the street, carrying my brown paper bag luggage when she called me over to her porch to find out what happened to my Star Wars pajama bottoms.

Mrs. Bourne didn't bother to call Mommie Dearest, probably because our shut-in mother had neglected to give out our phone number, but more likely because, days before, while Mrs. Bourne was weeding her vegetable garden she had witnessed Mommie Dearest plow through her terrified husband, for better or for worse, as she drove her Audi into the swimming pool. So instead of knocking on Mother's door, Mrs. Bourne called the Greenwich Police. Even though we surely would have been better off had Child Protective Services gotten involved, somehow someone got in touch with Moya who calmly explained everything thoroughly to the Police, even though they already knew what had happened since they had been called to investigate The Accident days before. The whole town knew for chrissakes since it made the front page of the *Greenwich Time*. After the funeral Moya moved in permanently and things got a little better.

WHEN I CALLED DADDY I used a payphone so he wouldn't recognize my number and banish me to voicemail like he had done every time since we last spoke. I lied to the mistrustful woman who answered and told her I was a florist with a delivery for Mr. Thompson but unfortunately I was unable to read the address on the card. When she asked who they were from I told her that I was not allowed to open the card as it was a federal crime, just like with mail. I don't think she believed me, even though it was the only thing I was being truthful about. After I got the address I picked up an anemic bouquet of sunflowers from a nearby bodega. They were my favorite and I thought it'd be nice if Daddy had something that I loved close to him, even if they were half-dead.

ALTHOUGH OUR STEPMOTHER lived only a handful of blocks away, Lower Manhattan was closed for business unless you had an ID proving that you weren't a terrorist who lived beneath 14th Street. I desperately pleaded with the cops at the police barricade, showing off the sunflowers and promising them I needed to check up on my dying father. They weren't buying it.

After several failed attempts I returned to Union Square, defeated. I lost myself amongst the posters of the lost, enjoying my misery amongst my missing company. It wasn't long before I began to wonder what kind of scheme you would have come up with to get past the police barricade.

I remembered being coked out of my head when you talked us into backstage passes to that *Garbage* concert at Roseland. You pulled something out of your ass about how we were conducting an interview for an underground *Garbage* fanzine that you aptly named *Dumpster*. We were shocked when the P.A. pulled us past the bouncer, gave us press passes and personally introduced us to Shirley Manson, who actually granted us a two-minute interview.

I was completely star-struck and couldn't do anything but gush, but you continued the charade flawlessly, yapping about how their electronic rhythms blended seamlessly with Shirley Manson's voice. You went on and on about how *Garbage's* rock-meets-electronic formula continued to combine aggression, sleek sexiness, and sonic polish in their latest album. About how their intricate soundscapes were magnificently assembled collages of sound. Shirley loved your B.S. so much that she actually gave you an unrestricted VIP access badge, but, of course, all you cared about was getting in good with the roadies so you could follow them into the back room and do more lines.

That's when I heard someone randomly call my name. I cringed, expecting to find you standing there until I remembered you were way too busy getting gang raped for the next few hours, possibly days. When I looked up I noticed a leggy blonde lugging her oversized Tumi roller bag through the park, waving at me. Her face was distorted by a white painters' mask and the luggage made her look like a tourist so I began to worry she might be some rabid *Big Brother* autograph hound. I was relieved, however, when the leggy blonde removed the white facial mask to reveal that she was actually Rollergirl from *Boogie Nights*. She was hard to recognize without her skates.

'Hey, Rollerbag Girl,' I smiled, not remembering her actual name, never remembering anybody's actual name no matter how famous or infamous they were. Rollergirl giggled and produced a spare white mask for me as she introduced me to that bitchy friend of hers who everyone else loved because she'd starred in all those repetitive Christopher Guest movies.

I'd met the Queen of the Indies several times before but she never seemed to remember me so I had to suffer through yet another humiliating introduction. The Indie Queen joked, as if she were as famous as Rollergirl, about how painter's masks were more effective at going incognito than a pair of oversized sunglasses and a baseball cap. The paper mask made me feel claustrophobic and I had trouble breathing, like I couldn't get enough oxygen, like I was asphyxiating myself, so I took it off and opted for the more abundant plastic-scented air.

I was riveted when Rollergirl filled me in about the terrorist attacks, but I didn't ask any questions because I didn't want her to think I was a pathetic Crackhead who was too self-involved to bother watching the news. I wanted to explain how you had kicked in the Porsche's stereo to the point where all it would play was the Daft Punk CD that we couldn't eject and listened to on repeat through twelve states. Funnily enough we never tired of it. Anyway.

Rollergirl me all about how her plane was actually flying in during the terrorist attacks. How she saw one of the Towers burning from first class. How she was on the very last plane given clearance to land at JFK before the second plane hit. How she had flown in to New York to close on a brand new co-op. How she witnessed the second tower get hit by a plane from the vantage point of her First Class window. How she watched the first tower fall while they were circling the airport waiting to be granted access to land. How she had been stuck on Long Island with her limo driver's family until the bridges opened yesterday. How once she got into Manhattan she wasn't allowed below 14th Street because she didn't have proof that she bought a new co-op there, 'So I checked into the W Hotel until I remembered that Parker lived in the East Village.'

'You look familiar,' the Indie Queen said, *again*. 'Didn't we meet at Heath's New Year's party?' I shrugged solely to irritate her and then played the lame, 'Nice to see you,' game before I asked, 'Could I tag along with you guys? I'm trying to get to 9th Street.'

I followed Rollergirl's roller bag toward the swarm of police officers guarding the blue barricades on 14th Street. The cops let the Indie Queen through when she produced her ID, but when Rollergirl and I tried to slip past the blue uniformed bouncer as if we were her +2 on the guest list, the cop wasn't having it. He demanded to see our California driver licenses then inspected mine for what seemed felt like an eternity before he shook his head with a mistrustful gaze and handed it back. Luckily the Indie Queen got up on her ever-present soapbox and said, 'We're celebrities, not terrorists!' I'm sure I didn't even register on the Cop's radar, but he was so enamored by Rollergirl's cleavage that he finally let us pass, but not before he inspected (and obviously got off on) the colorful panties in Rollergirl's roller bag.

The eerie silence below 14th kept us mute until we all gave each other double cheek kisses in front of some comic book store on Broadway. There were no cars, no horns, no sirens. Pedestrians behind the white masks were not talking and the stores were mostly shuttered. It reminded me of being stoned out of my mind during an eighth grade poetry lesson when Ms. Ramsey taught our moronic English class about oxymorons and used the pathetically cliché example of thunderous silence. After being hit below its 14th Street belt, lower Manhattan had definitely been silenced. City noise had been deafeningly replaced with American flags, proudly swaying outside apartment windows, defiantly hanging from air conditioners, and unapologetically spray-painted on top of American Apparel billboards. All the white masks tilted toward the heavens, abruptly yet in unison, when two Air Force F-16 fighter jets soared above us at a disturbingly low altitude, their thunderous jets replacing the oxymoronic silence while I began to wonder if we had begun World War III. And if so, who were we fighting?

I'D LOST ALL SENSE of time when I finally arrived at Daddy's building. His co-op building was called The Brevoort and it looked more like a massive hotel in that non-descript, post-war kind of way. Besides having an actual half-circular driveway which functioned as a taxi-turnabout, there was nothing remarkable about the light-colored, glazed brick building. Nothing besides the fact that it was where Daddy lived, where Daddy would die. It was hard to imagine that he spent the past twenty years in that luxury co-op while we spent the last twenty assuming he was living beneath his tombstone. While he *let* us assume he was buried. Why had he abandoned us like that? On the way to his funeral I vividly remembered asking Mommie Dearest why all the black cars kept their headlights on during the day, why everybody was wearing black, why we had to wear clip-on ties, why Daddy's body had to be buried underground. As usual, you couldn't have been less interested, even back then. I'm not even sure if you came. Even though you were three, you probably had something better to do that afternoon.

Thanks to an overwhelming feeling of déjà vu, my blood pressure rose as soon as I walked through the revolving doors. I desperately needed something to calm me down, something to slow my racing heart. Instead I was greeted by, 'Oh no. I don't fucking think so,' as the doorman dashed toward me from his post in the lobby. He kind of looked like Petey the Pit Bull from *The Little*

Rascals, mostly because he had this one black eye. His stance became sinister as he extended his arms into an impressive wingspan, similar to the crow on the soundstage just before it attacked. I pretended everything was Kosher, like I wasn't freaked out, like that was the way people typically greeted me. I ignored his defensive posturing and attempted to diffuse the bizarre situation with a simple smile. I held up the bouquet and said, 'Flower delivery for Thom Thompson in 9A.'

I was completely confused when he informed me, 'The Thompsons don't want nothing to do with the likes of you,' then he pushed me, full force, toward the door which hadn't actually stopped revolving from my attempted entrance. 'You ain't welcome here so get a move on cause the next black eye that gets doled out ain't gonna be for me.'

With that he literally threw me back through the revolving door with such force that it spun around and spat me onto the street. I continued my backward tumble and screamed when the swinging door caught my right ankle and practically took it on a solo trip back into the Lobby. I laid there, splayed along the sidewalk in such a way that I must've looked like a dead body waiting to be outlined in chalk.

There I was. Splayed out on the sidewalk surrounded by sunflower carcasses while my foot was caught in the revolving door of The Brevoort. Thankfully Petey the Pit Bull swung the door back in the opposite direction, not so much because he wanted to release my leg, but because he wanted to lock me out.

I limped toward the other, non-revolving door and tried to push my way through, barely getting my good foot inside before Petey the Pit Bull threw his body against it, denying my entrance with his excessive weight. Residents began to congregate in the lobby behind him, some elderly

Yentas excited by the unexpected drama, some Jimmy Choo-types annoyed by their unexpected shopping delay, but one thing was for sure, they were all looking at me. Recognizing me. Studying my face. Pointing and whispering.

'I think you must be mistaking me for my twin,' I said loudly through the glass door as I peered around the familiar yet completely foreign surroundings, 'I've never been here before.'

Petey the Pit Bull laughed at me and said, 'Fool me once, kid.'

I decided it was best to leave when he dialed 911, so I headed south into Washington Square Park to plan my next move. I tried calling Daddy several more times but nobody ever answered. I left several manic messages, possibly panicked, before I stumbled upon a friendly neighborhood drug dealer who sauntered by and kindly offered me, 'Coke 'n smoke,' under his breath.

Since you had stolen my cash and I had stolen your stash, I politely told him that I was all good and then promptly excused myself to the McDonald on West 3rd near Sixth to use the ATM and made good use of the rest room until one of the employees had to break in and kick me out.

6

I WAS STILL TWEAKING when the Metro-North conductor announced the station stop, 'Rivah-side!' The conductor spoke as if he were acting in some black-and-white movie with one of those 1950s affected New York accents that seem to have been derived from Central Casting. 'Station stop is *Rivah*-side! Next stop'll be Old Greenwich! *Ooold* Greenwich is next!'

My foot had fallen asleep while it was wedged tightly between the small area between the steel radiator and the seat in front of me. I jammed it there mostly to stop it from tapping. On at least three separate occasions the woman sitting in front of me turned around, severely irritated, and demanded me to stop kicking her seatback.

I felt bad, but the hubris in her tone had become increasingly annoying. I didn't understand why she wouldn't just move if I was being so bothersome. When she stood up I braced myself for another diatribe, but luckily she was only preparing to get off the train. Of course she was getting off at one of the Greenwich stops. The sound of her haughty voice was as pure-bred as Lauren Bacall's, trumped only by her pretentious choice of overly annunciated words, each dripping with an immense sense of entitlement. The fact that I was being bugged by this particular Lauren Bacall, a woman who was actually down-to-earth enough to have a job and, gasp, commute via public-transportation, was only a glaring sign that my 90210 sabbatical had obviously softened me from the old-moneyed ways of Greenwich.

I remained seated, partly because I didn't want to have another run in with Ms. Bacall, but mostly because I realized that it was not only my foot, yet my entire leg that had fallen asleep. I was afraid that I might actually fall over if I stood and draw unwanted attention to my inebriated state, so I suffered through the pins and needles and peered through the window at the eerie perfection of Greenwich. The only thing remotely ruffled by the breathtaking Monet-esque landscape were my nerves.

Sitting on the commuter train reminded me of that time you came home for one of your vacations after getting kicked out of yet another boarding school. It was long before either of us had come out, but somehow you convinced me into going to some downtown party at The Roxy which turned out to be this insanely gay nightclub.[29] We smoked some laced joint you bought from some lace-ridden drag queen in the ladies room and then, surprise, surprise, you disappeared. Somehow I got back to Grand Central where I had to wait until 5am for the next train while profusely throwing up in a public toilet near the Vanderbilt entrance while some homeless guy jerked off next to me. I fell asleep on the train and when the conductor woke me in Stamford he didn't seem to care that I had missed my stop, most likely because I had puked all over the seatback. You, of course, were nowhere to be found.

I walked along the tracks all the way back to Old Greenwich and was livid when I found you hiding out, crashed out in the loft area of Mommie Dearest's detached garage. You had been secretly living up there since you were no longer welcomed in the house, hidden away from the world as if you were Anne Frank, only without the

---

[29] A former roller disco, The Roxy began hosting dance nights in the 1980s and eventually turned into the "Studio 54 of roller rinks." Gayest club ever.

worthiness. I, of course, forgave you. Probably because I knew it was better to have you on my side than against me.

'Old Greenwich! Station stop is *Ooold* Greenwich!' The train slowed as it approached the platform and I stood up and my foot stumbled toward the exit on pins and needles. I shuffled onto the platform along with Ms. Bacall and all her various Brooks Brothers, all with leathered faces and matching briefcases swaying beneath their pinstriped sleeves.

I DECIDED TO WALK home from the train station, partly because I didn't feel up to dealing with the throng of people fighting over the two taxis, but mostly because I thought the walk would buy me some time to mentally prepare myself to see Mommie Dearest. It had been five years, give or take, since our last encounter. I walked down the train station's steps and then to the far end of the FoodMart parking lot before it filtered me through the golf course. You always claimed cutting through Innis Arden was the long way, even though it wasn't.

As I passed by the lower tennis courts I could hear squealing children from the pool on the hill and it reminded me of that time we stole a couple of six packs and broke in to go skinny dipping in the middle of the night. It was your idea, of course, since I was terrified of the water. Which, I'm sure, is exactly why you chose to go there. The pool was not lit, but there was a full moon that night and we had just enough light to sit on the adjacent diving boards and watch our empties sink into the deep end, one by one. You were up on the high dive, already pretty drunk by the time you began jumping up and down on the disturbingly flexible board. You went flying up into the air as if you were on a trampoline, obviously attempting to impress me with some exotic Greg Louganis-worthy dive, only without the abs.[30]

I begged you not to, pleaded with you about how I wouldn't be able to save you if something went wrong, that I couldn't swim, wouldn't swim, explained how you would surely drown. And that's when your foot missed the diving board, and your body flailed as something hit the edge of the board with a huge thud. You landed in an elaborate belly flop so loud it sounded as if you landed on concrete. I screamed as you laid on the water's surface in a full face-plant, lifeless. I knew you were trying to scare me, mostly because everything you did seemed to emanate from that same nasty motivation.

I screamed your name as you began to sink. Although the water was too dark to be sure, I was convinced that I could see blood pooling around your head. I was terrified. The thought of losing you was unbearable, unthinkable, but so was the thought of diving in after you and being responsible for your life. For your death. But of course I dove in. And then I panicked. I thought about The Accident. About Daddy. About how I was about to lose yet another family member to yet another unfortunate swimming pool accident. I couldn't see you even though I forced my head beneath the surface to search. I swallowed more water each time I gasped your name. My screams came out in a trickle of chlorine clogged coughs. It was late and no one could hear my frantic pleas.

That's when I felt something beneath me, probably because I kicked you, and I reached down one last time and felt your head. You were eerily motionless as I pulled you toward the surface by your hair. I tried to keep your

---

[30] Greg Louganis is an openly gay HIV+ American Olympic diver who swept the diving events in consecutive Olympic Games. The fact that he's gorgeous and wore skimpy bathing suits didn't hurt his scores a bit.

face out of the water as I doggie paddled us both to the pool ladder. I was still choking and didn't have the energy to pull myself out of the water, let alone both of us, but when I got situated with one hand on the ladder I used my free hand to hold your head and began to give you mouth-to-mouth. I was a wreck, screaming for help between deep breaths, then repeating the process. I don't know how long it went on before you slipped me the tongue and informed me, 'You're a terrible kisser.'

THE EXPENSIVE HOUSES barely visible through the trees and thick brush dotting the perimeter of the golf course were just as I'd left them. Almost as if I'd never left them. All the houses except, of course, ours. My heart dropped deep into my intestines, possibly my bowels, as our childhood home grew larger and more ominous with each step down the fairway. The house had become barely recognizable since my last visit. I couldn't help but think of how I worked to put so much time and distance between me and that horrific place, but there I was, ironically crawling back for answers to the very questions that drove us away in the first place.

It'd been almost twenty years since the last of the yard work had been done, as it'd been almost twenty years since Mommie Dearest murdered her chief landscaper, better known as Daddy. Or didn't murder him. Regardless, after decades of neglect the backyard was so overgrown that her once imposing Sea Captain's house was now only decomposing. The yard had become as unruly as her children and had taken on a decrepit quality that could simply be described as *Grey Gardens*. Which, of course, did nothing to ease my inner-Little Edie[31] about returning home.

Mommie Dearest took care of her property as diligently as she'd taken care of her children, but unlike us, the foliage had willingly stayed on to help insulate her from the outside world. Even looking at the decaying house was immobilizing. Trees, bushes, hedges and weeds had all melded together into one vine-like barricade, which I used to my advantage to camouflage my intrusion as I passed by Mommie Dearest's rusty 'No Trespassing' sign.

I wandered into the backyard, which felt more like the back-woods and accidentally stepped into a fetid puddle of God-knows-what as I made my way toward the detached garage. I hoped the back door key was still in its hiding spot since the only person who could've used it would have been you, but you were obviously much too busy being gang fucked at the W Union Square.

Although I had seen ancient pictures that proved we'd actually swum in it, besides being terrified of the water, I have nary a memory of ever having set foot into the black-bottomed pool which had long since evaporated. As expected, Mommie Dearest's Audi 5000 continued its rusty decay in the deep end which was also doubling as a massive nest to a bustling family of skunks, all of whom were curious about the estranged stranger walking through their backyard territory.

Nobody truly knows why she did it, but neighborhood lore of exactly how Mommie Dearest's Audi ended up in the pool was much more varied than the neighborhood demographic, which was as homogenous as the inbred skunks, only much, much whiter. Some say Mommie

---

[31] *Grey Gardens* is an endlessly quotable 1975 documentary film that depicts the everyday lives of two reclusive socialites, a mother and daughter both named Edith Beale (and both related to Jackie O), who lived in squalor at Grey Gardens, a decrepit mansion in the Hamptons with no running water and wild raccoons. "There are some nice people in the world, you know, I just don't happen to be related to any of them." --Little Edie

Dearest ran Daddy over because she caught him cheating. Others took the story further and thought Mommie Dearest was trying to kill herself along with our entire family. The only thing consistent about the stories was that Mommie Dearest was always the one who drove the Audi into its watery grave and always the one who ran Daddy over along the way. It was never proved, however. Years later Mommie Dearest got retribution when she settled a massive class action lawsuit against Audi, claiming that the car had magically accelerated even though her foot was pressed firmly upon the brake pedal. *60 Minutes* actually did a feature story on it, but of course Mommie Dearest refused to grant them an interview.

Much like the Audi which had been trapped happily-never-after in its new subterranean parking garage, Mommie Dearest had also become a prisoner inside her own decomposing home. Her incarceration, however, was voluntary.

ALTHOUGH THE STUMP formerly known as azalea bush had petrified since the last time I was home, the back door key was still beneath the cracked terracotta planter that entombed its carcass, exactly where you had hidden it a decade ago so we could sneak in and out, undetectable in the middle of the night.

That's when I got a knot in my stomach, so painful and tight that I began to wonder when I had last eaten, or taken a shit for that matter. But I had already begun my mission so there was no time for meals or bathroom breaks. Needless to say I decided to quell my body's pangs with what it desired most, and snuck into the detached garage to take advantage of its privacy. The idea of confronting

Mommie Dearest sober, or anything shy of completely fucked up, was completely out of the question.

The cobwebs in the garage caught me like an unsuspecting bug, enveloping me from head to toe. I panicked when it felt like something was crawling around on me and frantically searched for an angry black widow that was just as happy to welcome me into her lair as I was terrified to be there.

The only light crept through a filthy window and it took my eyes several moments to adjust to the darkness. The first thing that caught my eye was the cryptic blue Connecticut vanity plate, 'CVT LFE,' peeking out from beneath the blue tarp that we had stolen long ago from the Innis Arden Pro Shop to help protect the car from Mommie Dearest's leaking roof after your failed escape where you accidentally tore the convertible top off. I removed the tarp just enough so I could momentarily admire Mommie Dearest's steel prisoner before I yanked the Porsche's side view mirror completely out of its plastic housing and placed it on the hood.

I chopped up a nice rock into a long line on the mirror while staring speechless at my dead pupils. It wasn't long before the entire garage was illuminated with the turbo torch as I heated up the long glass cylinder until it began to glow like the Twinky Asian had taught me.

When the pipe was ripe enough I snorted the vaporized line off the side view mirror and was literally knocked onto the filthy garage floor in a ridiculous state of euphoria. I'm not sure exactly how long I laid there enjoying the jolt of elation, however I vividly recall bugging out on the afternoon sunlight that filtered through the dirty window, highlighting intricate patterns of the petrified spider web.

AFTER I LEFT the garage I was so light headed that I found myself having to hug the perimeter of the swimming pool's rusty fence for balance as I made my way toward Mommie Dearest's imposing backdoor. I was practically giddy as I attempted to keep a safe distance from several of the adorable fluffy black skunks, all with defensively risen rumps aimed in my direction.

Even though it'd only been less than four years since my last visit, the pathetic condition of the grounds was nothing short of astonishing. Masonry crumbled beneath my feet as I tentatively climbed the back steps. I inserted the key into the familiar door, which, similar to the rings of a tree-trunk, exposed its age through various colorful layers of chipping paint. I unlocked the door and entered the large mudroom adjacent to the kitchen. It felt as if I'd never left. Although the yard outside had become as imposing as Hansel and Gretel's forest, the interior of the house was far from a witch's lair. Everything was absolutely spotless, as if no time had passed. Well, no time since the last renovation in the mid-seventies, just before we were born.

Unlike most places I'd revisited as an adult, everything in Mommie Dearest's house seemed bigger than I remembered. I walked through the cavernous kitchen which was probably several square feet larger than that sixth-floor walk-up we'd rented in Hell's Kitchen. I began to wonder if Moya was still alive but my rhetorical question was answered by the immaculate state of Mommie Dearest's matching, olive-colored appliances.

I tiptoed up the backstairs, partly because I was terrified, but mostly so as not to lose the element of surprise when I entered the lion's den. I even took my shoes off as I walked across the creaky floorboards that comprised the upstairs hall landing. The windows gleamed from the inside, yet were obscured to the point of being practically opaque after decades of grimy buildup on the exterior.

Oddly, I found myself mesmerized by the surroundings of my peculiar childhood. I could barely make out the ancient headstones next door in the Tomac cemetery, the oldest graveyard in the entire town of Greenwich, which dated back to the seventeenth century. It was so old that the thin headstones had weathered long past the point of being readable. Neighborhood kids were terrified of it. Most would cross the road and hold their breath when they passed by. Ironically I always enjoyed living next door to an ancient cemetery that went defunct centuries ago. After Daddy died I found a certain comfort in being surrounded by death. And while I was peering out the filthy window I found myself surprised by the fact that I had any sort of appreciation for anything about Mommie Dearest's house, even its all-encompassing views of human decomposition. But it soon became overwhelmingly obvious that, like most everything, my childhood traumas were much more palatable after a crystalicious side of Tina.

BILL HEMMER'S sexy voice emanated from the tinny speaker of Mommie Dearest's antique, seventeen inch Sony Trinitron and gave me courage to peek through her bedroom door. Or rather, encouraged me. CNN was reporting on the collapse of the Twin Towers and the missing people, presumably dead. I was so shocked to see footage of commercial airliners actually slicing through the iconic buildings that I accidentally gasped and blew my cover.

'Who's there?' Mommie Dearest slurred, obviously she was just as fucked up as I was, if not moreso.

I took a huge breath before I mustered up enough courage to walk into her bedroom and explain the reason for my surprise visit, my surprise attack.

The room was like a morgue. It felt more antiseptic than clean, as if Mommie Dearest was more of Moya's patient than her employer. The curtains were drawn and she was lying on top of her ancient bedspread, wearing the same threadbare terrycloth bathrobe she'd worn as long as I can remember. She greeted me with all the subdued exhilaration of a housebound, decades-long valium addict when she asked, 'Well, well, well. Isn't this just too precious?' Mommie Dearest muted her TV and began to speak nonsensically.

Even though she was barely present, her presence still knocked the wind out of me. Mommie Dearest looked older than I remembered, less formidable. I was rendered mute when she slurred, 'What's that you're fiddling with in your pants pockets?'

I, of course, embarrassedly retrieved my hands from an unconscious game of pocket pool and evaded her question by asking another. The very question which brought me across the country in the first place, 'Why did you lie to us about Daddy being dead?'

'What on earth are you talking about?' And then, as was always to be expected with liars, Mother changed the subject entirely, 'You're too thin. Will you be staying for lunch? I don't eat much anymore but we'll have to inform Moya if you'll be staying.

If nothing else, hot railing meth was keeping me highly focused. Instead of saying something hurtful like, 'You've put on weight,' or even politely declining her luncheon invitation, I repeated myself, only louder and slower, like an ugly American demanding to be understood in a foreign country. 'Why did you lie to us about Daddy being dead?'

'You're not making any sense, Thompson. Is something wrong? You don't look well.'

When it came to conversations with our troubled mother, I found it was best not to divulge any more information than was absolutely necessary. 'Yes, Mommie Dearest, something is very wrong.'

'Why do you insist on calling me that? Show some respect for your old mother.'

'Have another valium, Mommie Dearest.'

'Is that supposed to upset me? Surely you can do better than that. The whole world already knows I'm a horrible pill-head of a mother. You made that abundantly clear while you were on *Big Brother*,' her saccharine voice had finally reached her patented, tranquilized *Stepford Wives*[32] tone typically reserved for unwelcomed telemarketers and her children.

'I'm surprised you bothered to watch.' And I really was.

'I'm surprised you're surprised. Besides what else have I got to do around here but watch television?' she said nonchalantly.

Then there was this endless pause where both of us came to a stubborn standstill for no other reason than an historical unwillingness to expose our double bluff. But, being in a speedy, chatty mood, I lost the challenge. 'Why did you tell us Daddy was dead when he wasn't?'

And just like that she dropped her decades long bluff, 'I thought it was for the best. Things got very confusing after The Accident. You wouldn't understand.'

'I was in the car when you ran him over. Try me.'

'My relationship with your father was very complicated. The fact that I tried to kill him had nothing to do with you.'

'Nothing to do with me? He was my father!'

---

[32] *The Stepford Wives* is a 1975 science fiction–thriller cult film about a town where all the wives are replaced by perfectly polite robots who live to serve their husbands. The film was remade in 2004 as a comedy and it is, to date, the most dreadful thing Nicole Kidman has ever starred in. And I don't mean dreadful in a good way.

Her attention turned back to the television and I was no longer sure who she was talking about, 'It's just so tragic. I don't know how any one person could be so evil and cause such destruction.'

'That's ironic.'

I had finally struck a heavily medicated nerve. She glared at me and hissed, 'What is all *this* about anyway?' she asked, shaking her hand all about as if she was doing the Hokey Pokey.

'What exactly do you mean by *this?*' I parroted her annoying gesture.

'The breaking and entering. The Spanish Inquisition. Honestly, I never know what you expect from me.'

'How about the truth for a change? Why did you lie about Daddy being dead?'

'Who told you he was alive?'

'He did. He called me. He told me he was dying.'

Concern peered through her heavily medicated eyes, 'Your father is dying? Which one?'

'What do you mean which one?'

'Who called you?' She screamed at me and I stared at her incredulously for a long beat, scanning her face for telltale signs of lucidity, before I responded tentatively in the form of a question, 'Daddy called me?'

I'm not sure exactly how, but my confusion had a definite calming effect on her, 'That's too bad.'

Then I informed her, 'I'm going to find him.'

'I don't know why you'd bother. The man is not even your real father,' the words fell from her lips as if she was throwing out trash. I had no idea if she was semi-coherent or if she had slipped back into Valium-land. Was she covering up old lies with new ones? Or had I accidentally fallen face first into the truth?

'What are you talking about?' I demanded.

'The man you think of as your father is not actually your father.'

'How is that even possible,' I demanded.

'When I got pregnant I told him that he was the father and he proposed. It's as simple as that. Now can we change the subject?'

'No we cannot change the subject, Mother!'

'Honestly, Thom, you're exhausting me.'

'Did you not think I'd have a few questions after you drop the bomb on me that the man I thought was my father is not?'

'I shouldn't have said anything.'

'Of course you should have. Only you might have said something eighteen years ago instead of telling me he was dead! Who is my real father?'

'I'm sorry Thompson, but I really can't do this anymore. Shall I have Moya make up the guest room for you?' She shook a few pills from one of the many prescription bottles on her nightstand and swallowed them whole, without water, as if they were nourishment. Mommie Dearest was shutting me out via medication and I didn't know what to say, what to ask in order to get closer to the answers I craved, the information I deserved. And my window of opportunity was closing almost as quickly as Mommie Dearest's medicated eyelids.

Although I don't remember much from our childhood, I still remember Daddy's funeral as if it were yesterday. It had been the worst day of my miserable little life. Mommie Dearest dressed up in matching Brooks Brothers' suits and I cried the entire time. You, on the other hand, were eerily silent. I remember wondering if you actually understood what had happened, even though I wasn't even sure that I understood that Mommie Dearest murdered Daddy, that he was never coming back? But I didn't want to explain it to you. Kind of like in second grade at the Old Greenwich

School playground when David Rabinowitz told me the truth about Santa Claus during recess. Although Santa had long since stopped visiting our house, I still felt duped. Like Mommie Dearest herself had been at the very center of the entire Kris Kringle conspiracy. I can't remember why you weren't at school that day, but I do remember racing home to inform you. Luckily, Moya found me as I raced through the back door, crying. She kept probing me with questions until I cracked and explained how I felt like it was my duty to tell everyone about the awful injustice being played out on children all over the world. I was practically hysterical.

Moya told me it was my decision. Since I knew the truth it was obviously up to me to tell whomever I wanted. But then she explained that whoever I told might feel just as sad as me. Did I want that on my conscience? She told me that sometimes it was better to pretend and go on like something horrible never happened. Although Moya never graduated from High School, she remains, to this day, the smartest person I've ever known.

MY MIND RACED as I tried to figure out a way to get answers to my questions. Why hadn't Mommie Dearest left her house for twenty years? Why did she run over Daddy and then lie that he was dead? And now, who is our real father? And for that matter, who the hell was our fake one? I wondered if she just made everything up to throw me off her scent. I knew I had stumbled into something big, but I wasn't sure if it was just a big pile of shit.

The hot rails helped me focus and boil all my queries down into one simple question. The mother of all questions. For our mother. For Mommie Dearest. But when it came out of my mouth, surprisingly it was neither emotional nor campy. In fact, when I asked, 'Why did you have children?' it came out quite earnest.

Then there was this brief, ice-clinking-against-the-tumbler moment as Mommie Dearest took a sip of something. Although clear, it clearly wasn't water. For a moment it seemed like she was considering how best to answer my question, but then she said, 'I think it's time for you to go. I'm not feeling well today. But thank you so much for dropping by, Thompson. Keep in touch.' A slight quiver in her voice amplified her ambivalence as she inspected decades of water damage on the ceiling which Moya was obviously too short and stout to clean or repair.

I couldn't take it anymore. I became combative and raised my voice. 'Don't patronize me. Just answer the damn question and I'll go. Why would a sick and demented person like you ever decide to have children?' I crossed a line, but it was necessary to snap her back to reality. I stared at her coldly, searching her watery blue eyes for the slightest hint of presence.

Vodka dripped from her wet lips like poison as she said venomously, 'You're right, Thompson, I never wanted to have you. Having you ruined my life. Ruined your father's life. Ruined the entire family. Unfortunately I was living in denial and didn't have the guts to take care of it myself.'

She said 'Take care of it' as if she were getting a dog neutered, but that wasn't half as odd as the fact that she had referred to me us as 'it.' She had temporarily emerged from a decade's long, self-medicated coma and she was bitter. I knew she intended for her words to destroy me, but on the contrary they did nothing but empower me,

'Thank you for your honesty. Now if you would just tell me who my real father was I promise to never bother you again.'

Then through streaming tears she ordered, 'I forbid you to find him!' Her pleas quickly built from, 'I'm trying to protect you,' into a melodramatic, 'I'm begging you. Please don't look for him! Nothing good will come from it.' And then she closed her lame argument with a sullen, 'People have a right to their privacy.'

'People should think of that before they waive their right to birth control and abortion.'

'Don't be a son-of-a-bitch, Thompson!' It was always a bit disarming when Mother called me that. As you very well know, when Mommie Dearest got angry she'd typically say 'Fudge' or 'Sugar,' with such virulence that they'd long ago lost any implied sweetness to me. But 'son-of-a-bitch' was the only curse word Mother ever used. And its use was reserved specifically for her actual sons.

'Why do you always call me that? My whole life I've never heard you utter a single curse word. Ever. Yet for some perverse reason you seem to get great pleasure in calling me a son-of-a-bitch.'

'Are we done?'

'Not quite. As usual you've successfully evaded all my questions, but now I'd really like to know why any mother would refer to her son as a son-of-a-bitch?'

'This has become a grueling conversation, Thompson.'

'When you think about it, it's really quite self-deprecating.'

A slight quiver in her voice was the only indication of her ambivalence when the venom spat out of her mouth, 'Because you are a son-of-a-bitch!'

MOMMIE DEAREST'S sewing room was exactly as I remembered, hideous floral wallpaper and all. It felt like a hot set, painstakingly recreated on a soundstage for a long running series where I was barely an extra. Like a homing pigeon I raced toward the built-in cabinets to search through the endless set of pretentious, hard-bound books which hadn't been touched by anything other than Moya's feather duster since they'd been shipped over on the Mayflower. I scanned the books until, out of the corner of my eye, I noticed it tucked away, deep within the recessed shelving. Our baby book. It was hard to believe Mommie Dearest had held onto it all those years, given her obvious lack of feeling for sons of bitches.-

My curiosity took over and I began to flip through the pages. I was especially surprised by the level of detail, the sheer amount of effort she put into filling out the minutia on each and every page. Flipping through the diary Mommy Dearest kept of our infancy, one might assume she was more maternal than resentful, more protective than psychotic. In fact, had I been a soap opera star suffering from a convenient case of amnesia, I might have actually been fooled into thinking that, at one point, Mommie Dearest had actually enjoyed raising children.

I kept flipping pages, mesmerized by elaborately descriptive sentences on each and every page. There were whole paragraphs. All about us. I found snippets of once blonde hair saved from our first haircuts, foot prints from the hospital where we were born, and pages and pages of boring-ass baby blah-blah. In fact, it was so surprising that I found myself inspecting the handwriting because I began to wonder if perhaps Daddy had been the one who filled it out? Or possibly Moya since she was the one who actually raised us? But Mommie Dearest's flowery penmanship was unmistakable. Her distinctive A's and M's kept me turning pages as I tried to imagine the endless amount of time she must have taken to record all our boring-ass baby shit.

After I flipped past one particularly innocuous page, I stumbled upon exactly what I had expected in to find in the first place: absolutely nothing. And every page after the empty one was full of more and more nothing, because nothing more was ever recorded. Keepsakes were no longer attached by yellowed Scotch tape whose adhesive had long since dried up. There were no more first fingernail clippings, first teeth, or first poops. No more information was ever recorded from the time we were three years old. From the time of The Accident. Yet, surprisingly everything, absolutely everything up until that particularly fateful day seemed like it had been recorded by an obsessive-compulsive historian. If we weren't the living and breathing evidence, I might have wondered if perhaps we'd died some sort of sudden crib death.

I was anxiously flipping through the book when I eventually stumbled upon exactly what I had been searching for: our birth certificates. I scanned mine and was shocked when I read his name. For once Mommie Dearest was not lying because the man listed as our father was definitely not Thom Thompson, Junior. But I was even more shocked when I realized it was a name I had heard before. It was the same name that we found on that prescription bottle years ago: Jackson Zapf. I was overtaken by a sudden chill which shivered its way through goose pimples even though it was still hot and stuffy outside.

When I heard Moya say, 'Look what the cat done drag in…' I shoved the birth certificate into my pocket and placed the book back on the shelf.

Moya was a little older and a lot bigger than I remembered, yet her eyes still had that same familiar twinkle. My dilated pupils immediately darted away for protection, desperately looking for an escape hatch. Moya began to tap her cheek with her index finger, signaling that I'd best stop whatever the hell I thought I was doing and show some respect, in the form of a kiss, to the woman who had raised me. Although she was the only person who'd always been there for me, for us, the sight of her did nothing but incite panic. Instead of greeting her, I fled past her in a vain attempt to free myself from the childhood I had, moments ago, decided to replace.

BY THE TIME I made it to the hallway I was trembling so severely that I missed a step and practically tripped down the front stairs. I steadied myself by grabbing onto the staircase's recently polished cherry handrail, then slipped across the threadbare hand knotted Persian rug, dashing toward the oversized front door, my last obstacle before emancipation. Seeing Mommie Dearest was difficult enough, but the last thing I wanted to do was deal with an endless interrogation from Detective Moya. I unlocked the door chain and yanked spastically on the brass handle, trying desperately to release the horribly warped door from its tight frame, which, thanks to years of weather combined with the humidity, proved impossible. Harsh jerks caused the door knocker to clang as if some spastic peddler was trying to gain entrance. I don't know how long I had been yanking on it, praying for it to open, before I heard Moya scold me from behind, 'Boy, ain't you forgetting something? Or are you too big and famous to bother sayin' hello to an old maid?'

My shortness of breath was overshadowed by my racing heart, so when Moya pulled me into a bear hug, emotionally I had no choice but to burst into tears. Everything was way too fucking overwhelming. She attempted to calm me with a stream of maternal whispers like, 'It's okay, baby. Let it all out. Moya's here now.'

I did my breathing exercises to calm my heart while I was sandwiched between Moya's bosom and the beveled woodwork of the useless door. She squeezed me tighter and wrung the words right out of me.

'Why did Mommie Dearest lie about Daddy being dead?'

Moya covered her eyes guiltily, 'Lord have mercy.'

'You knew he was alive?'

'Your mother swore me to secrecy. And I honestly thought it was for the best. How did you find out?'

'He called me.' There was a long beat before I asked, 'Did you helped her fake his funeral?'

Moya stared at me in disbelief for a moment before she removed herself from the equation, 'Who's funeral?'

'Daddy's. I remember you were there with me.'

'Child, how on earth could I have been there if it never happened?'

'I'm telling you, that bitch faked his funeral!'

Moya pushed me away with a reprimand, 'You ain't too old for me to wash out that filthy mouth with some Ivory soap. Especially after all those horrible things you said on *Big Brother*. A son should never talk about his mother like that. It ain't right.'

'I'm going to find Daddy.'

She shook her head as she let me slip away, beneath her arm, and I hurried out the kitchen door to make my escape.

I FELT MORE TRAPPED when I made it outside, mostly due to my lack of transportation options. As usual, the suburbs had me shackled and I couldn't stand the torture of being in Greenwich for another moment. The sound of tweeting birds and chirping crickets combined with the smell of the Tomac Avenue cemetery's freshly cut grass was nothing less than stifling. I paced back and forth along Mommie Dearest's weed-ridden, white-pebbled drive and began to concentrate on my dwindling options.

That's when Moya opened the backdoor and yelled, 'Why don't you come inside and fill me in on every last bit of Hollywood gossip so's I can fix you some of my famous buttermilk hotcakes? Your skinny rear-end looks like it could use a home cooked meal.' At that point I was sure of nothing besides the fact that I was absolutely not hungry, even though I couldn't remember the last time I had a meal.

I ignored Moya and dialed 411 instead. I begged the operator to connect me to Greenwich Taxi as I attempted to hatch an escape plan, pacing back and forth when, ironically, I literally tripped over it. Weeds pushed through what was left of the white pebbled driveway and had camouflaged the steel link chain that emanated from the garage and looped around the giant Chestnut tree, before it disappeared back under the garage door.

I had just opened the garage when the Greenwich Taxi dispatcher finally answered. I found myself having an *American Psycho* moment but instead of disseminating useless information about Huey Lewis as if I were Patrick Bateman,[33] I began to rattle off random Porsche trivia. I told the dispatcher everything I knew about the vintage car's history, 'In 1981 when I was a year old the first Porsche 911 Cabriolet concept car was introduced at the Frankfurt Motor Show. Not only was the car a true convertible, but it also featured four-wheel drive—

---

[33] Patrick Bateman is a fictional character, the antihero and narrator of the novel *American Psycho* by Bret Easton Ellis, and was played by Christian Bale in the film adaptation. Patrick is a successful investment banker on Wall Street, however in his "secret life" Bateman is a serial killer who murders a variety of people, from colleagues, to the homeless, to prostitutes. His crimes, including rape, torture, murder, necrophilia and cannibalism, are described in graphic detail in the novel.

although that was dropped in the production version. The first 911 Cabriolet debuted in late 1982, although as a 1983 model. It was Porsche's first cabriolet since the 356 of the mid-1960s and it proved very popular with over four-thousand sold in its introductory year, despite its premium price relative to the open-top Targa.'

The dispatcher said, 'That's fascinating, kid. Do you need a taxi, or what?'

The Patrick Bateman in me tried to imagine the expression on the dispatcher's face as I yanked his small intestines from his freshly filleted abdomen, squeezing them tightly in my fist until they began to expose his unhealthy breakfast choices. Then I told him politely, 'No, thank you,' and simply hung up the phone.

THE MANUAL GARAGE door had practically rusted shut, and it was so ridiculously difficult to open that it actually winded me. A skunk ran out and gave me the evil eye, but was obviously happy for his newfound freedom and chose not to spray me.

Although the classic car was covered in dust and spider webs, now that it was exposed to daylight Daddy's 1983 fire engine red, Porsche 911 SC Cabriolet still took my breath away. It was even more beautiful than the rented one that Rosie Perez's Brother had towed away earlier that morning. This one was the original. A true classic.

The tires were mostly flat, but I quickly deemed that they were temporarily road-worthy, at least until I could get some air into them at Mackey's service station on Sound Beach.

I wandered around the car, admiring it, inspecting it, stroking it, until Moya reappeared, obviously keeping tabs on me.

'What's goin' on out here that could possibly be more fascinating than my famous buttermilks?'

I neglected to answer since I was far too busy scrutinizing the galvanized steel chain that shackled the lifeless convertible. Mommie Dearest had carefully sewn the chain through the passenger door handle, through the open window, and then switched to a needlepoint stitch, awkwardly knitting the chain through each of the steel beams that made up the skeleton of the convertible top. She had made one last loop through the steering wheel before the chain exited through the driver-side window and was reintroduced to its other end and padlocked around the chestnut tree. Thank God she had been too overmedicated to wrap it around anything substantial like an axel, because then I would've been fucked.

I KNEW IT WAS POINTLESS to try to pry information about Daddy from the heavy-set, Fort Knox of a woman who raised me, so I went back to inspect the Porsche's restraints and calculate my options. I thought about driving away as fast as I could until the chain gave way, but that plan had not worked out so well for you and I was slightly more apprehensive about damaging the collectible car than the grim possibility of being decapitated by the snapping chain. I'd fantasized about making this exact dramatic escape ever since you'd attempted it a decade ago, freeing both myself as well as the unjustly imprisoned Porsche.

My heart began to race when Moya stepped in front of the car to block my exit. She screamed something about how I was in no shape to drive (which was obviously true, yet completely moot if the car wouldn't start). I hopped into the driver's seat and turned the key which Mommie

Dearest had left in the ignition of the leashed car just to taunt us. My decapitation fantasy faded when the ignition offered nothing in return for the slight twist of my wrist. The battery had obviously died soon after you tried to steal it, probably sometime during the Ronald Regan, trickle-down economics era.

I BECAME ANTSY waiting for Triple A to arrive. Since I was highly focused on freeing Daddy's turbocharged prisoner I began to search through the garage for anything that might cut through galvanized chain. The ax barely made a nick. Neither did the rusty pruning shears I found hanging near the Lawn Boy mower which hadn't been used since Bonnie Tyler's heart had totally eclipsed. The chainsaw, however, was at least fun to use, mostly because the noise and sparks gave the whole experience a *Friday the 13th* meets *Flashdance* quality. It also had the added benefit of scaring Moya back into the house after I waved it around. She threatened to call the Greenwich police but I knew that would never happen since Mommie Dearest would never agree to any situation that might result in her having to leave her self-imposed house arrest.

I briefly considered my options. Since the convertible top had already been decapitated, my choices were to saw off the remaining parts of the Porsche that Mommie Dearest had strung the chain through—namely the passenger side door handle and the steering wheel—but I ultimately decided that it would be difficult to drive without a steering wheel.

Ultimately I opted for Plan B and walked toward the old chestnut tree while yanking the chainsaw's cord until it roared back to life.

THE CHAINSAW had only cut halfway through the oversized tree trunk by the time Triple A arrived, so I had to put my Paul Bunyon routine on the back burner in order to force Mommie Dearest's rusted driveway gate open wide enough for the tow truck to enter. Moya came running outside when she noticed the supersized stranger lugging orange jumper cables around his neck like a life preserver. My life preserver.

Instinctively I looked up to the bay window in Mommie Dearest's bedroom, and of course she was standing there, as ominous as if she were Norman Bates pretending to his mother.[34] I ignored her and escorted the tow truck driver into the garage while attempting to convince him that neither Moya nor her desperate threats of 'aiding and abetting a car thief' were of any concern to him. I flashed my Triple A card along with a twenty and assured him, 'You're free to go after you start the car.'

Although initially hesitant, the ignition finally succumbed to encouraging words and rhythmic prods to the gas pedal. Finally the motor turned over and began to purr like a neglected alley cat who'd stumbled onto the set of Fancy Feast commercial shoot.

I thanked the Tow Truck driver with another twenty and promised him I'd let the Porsche's battery charge for a bit before I stole it.

Moya was like my shadow. She begged me to reconsider my increasingly obvious plan, bellowing over the noisy chainsaw as I began my second cut into the tree trunk, slightly above the first, as if I were slicing an enormous piece of homemade Chestnut-tree pie.

---

[34] Norman Bates is a fictional character created by writer Robert Bloch as the main character in his novel *Psycho*, and portrayed by Anthony Perkins as the primary antagonist of the 1960 film of the same name directed by Alfred Hitchcock. In a nutshell Norman has a few mother issues and often dresses up as his dead mother to kill people that stay in his motel.

The crackling began before the second cut intersected with the first. I threw the chainsaw aside and jumped behind the tree in order to push it in the direction that I wanted it to fall. Toward the house. *On* the house. Although I wasn't much of a lumberjack, my plan was that the falling tree would tear through the back walls of Mommie Dearest's prison and reveal its internal workings as if it were a doll house, exposing all its dysfunction.

Unfortunately my aim was way more than slightly off. The tree came down with a deafening crackle before it fell and covered the empty pool, crashing down upon the Audi's carcass as frightened skunks fled from the scene of my landscaping crime.

THANKS TO MY FAILED, yet rather noisy attempt at gardening, the neighbors began to congregate in the street and gossip. I ignored them while collecting the excess galvanized steel chain and threw the heavy pile into the Porsche's backseat. My heart raced as I hopped into the dusty car and popped the clutch. The car lunged forward with all the pent up energy of a horny convict whose rape sentence had been overturned thanks to new DNA evidence.

Moya, of course, stood in the driveway, hands on hips as if her stern stance could deter my getaway. I felt bad about doing it, yet had no choice. With the clutch fully engaged I punched the gas and revved the engine as if I were racing the Indy 500. The car didn't move an inch but my bluff sent old Moya diving for cover, ultimately disappearing into a tall stalk of weeds. Once she was safely out of the way, I popped the clutch.

It wasn't long before Daddy's Porsche was spitting white pebbles in its wake as it tore out of Mommie

Dearest's weed-infested driveway. Even though my *Thelma and Louise* moment was Louise-less,[35] I squealed gleefully as the newly freed convertible roared past the nosy neighbors. The sleepy little town of Old Greenwich had obviously not seen such a dramatic performance since Mommie Dearest had driven her Audi into the swimming pool, almost two decades ago. Even Mrs. Burgess and her eldest son with Down's Syndrome came out to enjoy the neighborhood spectacle.

---

[35] *Thelma & Louise* is a 1991 film with feminist overtones starring Geena Davis, Susan Sarandon and Brad Pitt. After several run-ins with low-life men the duo find themselves trapped between the Grand Canyon and a hard place. Rather than be captured and spend the rest of their lives in jail, they gleefully drive over the cliff while they reminisce about Brad Pitt's abs.

5

DRIVING DADDY'S vintage Porsche was like nothing I'd ever experienced. Although the car wasn't nearly as fast or slick as the new one Adam, um, rented, the original cabriolet had undeniable character which made the driving experience, although flawed by years of neglect, feel flawless.

The 1983 cabriolet was equipped with a state-of-the-art, Dolby digital cassette deck, but the only tape I found was far less groundbreaking. I sang along to *We Are Detective* until I couldn't take the irony any longer. I remembered when you made Daddy buy the tape at Caldor's because you thought that the *Thompson Twins* must have named their band after us, even though the British trio were neither twins, nor named Thompson. I ended up drowning them out with a single stomp of my right foot as I opened up the engine to clean out the clogged fuel injectors. I flew past the Innis Arden Clubhouse, and it wasn't long before I rediscovered 92.7 WLIR. I couldn't get that new Kylie song outta my head as I gassed up at Mackey's and added air to the ailing tires.

I CRUISED AROUND Binney Park a few times, attempting to charge the battery a bit before I pulled over and let it idle in order to take the edge off with a quick hit from the pipe. Since you had destroyed the convertible top years ago, I crouched down deep into the bucket seat to cloak my illegal actions. While exhaling a very nice puddle, I found myself drawn to our new father's familiar yet completely foreign name on my birth certificate. It wasn't long before I had smoked enough courage to dial information. The automated operator asked, 'City and listing please?'

'Greenwich, Connecticut. I think. Actually I'm not really sure where he lives, but his real name is...' I paused dramatically, mostly because it was the first time I'd ever tried to pronounce the name aloud, 'Jackson Zapf.' I began to wonder what he looked like as I waited and hoped that the operator would find a phone number to connect us.

That's when a Greenwich Police patrol car crawled up beside me. In my peripheral vision I could tell that the cop in the passenger seat was intently eyeballing me. He was overly interested in the vintage Porsche and it's missing top to such a degree that I began to worry that Mommie Dearest had reported it stolen. The cop's presence was overshadowed by excitement when an actual human operator came back with the information I had almost forgotten I'd asked for, 'I have a Jackson Zapf located in Stamford.'

'Really?'

'Would you like the number?'

'Um...Yes, please,' I said as I nodded carefully back to the officer while casually slipping the pipe beneath the driver's seat.

My heart pounded as the cops drove away and the human operator and was replaced by a computerized voice which prompted me to, 'Press one to connect to (203)...'

Ecstatic, I pressed 'one' before the robotic voice was able to recite the phone number. I didn't realize how unprepared I was to have a conversation until a woman answered and I found myself speechless. The woman kept repeating, 'Hello? *Hello?*' and even though my mind was racing, my dry tongue was frozen. Her raspy New York accent was thicker than *The Nanny's*,[36] yet she was completely unintelligible because she was chomping on what sounded like a cud of Nicorette gum. After more than a few uncomfortable chomps, I simply hung up because I had no idea what to say.

MY CELL RANG instantaneously and startled me so much that I answered without bothering to check the incoming number, 'Hello?'

The raspy voice chewed me out, 'Star-sixty-nine works on blocked numbers, ya know.'

I chuckled because it was as equally amusing as it was obnoxious and I quickly found myself thinking of how it would be something that you would have done. 'Sorry, I have a lousy cell signal,' I lied. 'I guess you couldn't hear me.'

She laughed and said, 'Sawwww-reeeeeeeeee!' in an irritating, yet completely endearing way.

I asked, 'Is Jackson Zapf there?' barely able to pronounce my fake father's overly consonant-ed name.

She asked 'Who's calling, please?' as if she was reenacting Lily Tomlin's One-Ringy-Dingy sketch.[37]

'This is Thom Thompson.'

'That's quite the name. Hold one moment please.' The raspy voice muffled the phone receiver with her palm which I imagined to be connected to five very long, overly polished Lee Press-On's. My pulse raced impatiently as I began to panic about what the hell I would say to Jackson

---

[36] Fran Drescher is an American film and television actress, comedian, producer, and activist. She is best known for her role as Fran Fine in the hit TV series, *The Nanny,* her nasal voice and thick New York accent. After working on the show for three seasons I assure you, that is Fran's real voice.
[37] Lily Tomlin's character Ernestine was a nosy, condescending telephone operator with a penchant for snorting and treating her customers badly.

Zapf when he finally came to the phone. At this point I was sure of nothing.

My heart began to pound with emotional pangs for the only father we'd actually known, yet had long since forgotten. I began to reminisce about him getting ready for work in the morning, knotting ties, putting on his black rubbers to protect his leather shoes from the rain. I remembered Daddy climbing the old pine tree behind the garage without changing out of his work suit because we were in an emotional frenzy over saving the Kirchner's screaming Siamese kitten which had gotten stuck. I thought about Daddy covering our little bodies with buckets of sand and building elaborate race cars around us at Tod's Point, complete with clam shell steering wheels and racing stripes made of seaweed; about how we would pretend to drag race until the rising tide washed our sand cars away, along with any more recent memory of Daddy.

Finally there was a click on the line and suddenly the man who shared none of these memories with me said, 'This is Jack Zapf.'

I gulped and said something profound like, 'Hi.'

'Can I help you?' he said, most likely annoyed.

'I'm trying to locate Jackson Zapf.'

'Well, I'm afraid you've found him. Unless, of course, you're selling something?' he chuckled with an accent that was much less objectionable than the woman who answered the phone who may or may not have been our sister.

'No, no, no. Nothing like that,' I lied, instantly realizing that it was exactly like that. I was selling myself to Jackson Zapf. Selling him a son.

'What did you say your name was?'

'Thom. Thom Thompson.'

'Is this some kind of joke?'

'Not at all. I think I might be your son.'

Jackson's heavy silence clued me into the fact that I had found the right man, whoever he was. I attempted to gather my courage into words so I could continue stirring up Mommie Dearest's pot of chaos that she'd been stewing for years.

The syncopation of our breath filled the stillness with anticipation and familiarity. The only sound came from the symphony of insects which seemed to swell through Binney Park like a stadium full of crazed fans doing the wave. During the lengthy silence I found myself stockpiling questions: what did he look like, why did he leave us and what kind of car did he drive? I wondered if he had lost all his hair? But mostly I wondered whether Jackson Zapf was our real father? I needed someone to look like me. Someone who wasn't you.

Unfortunately the air that had previously filled my lungs, as well as my sails, was quickly replaced by a heart-wrenching vacuum as Jackson Zapf said, 'Please don't ever call here again,' and then hung up.

I IMMEDIATELY CALLED 411 again but this time I requested an address for Jackson Zapf. Luckily he was conveniently located just over the Stamford border on Fairfield Avenue. But since street names were as elusive to me as people's names, I had no idea where it was. The thought of driving around Stamford until I stumbled upon it seemed more time consuming than buying a map or even finding an internet café where I could print out directions without having to talk to anyone. Ultimately I stumbled upon a Radio Shack in the Riverside Shopping Center and impulsively bought a portable GPS unit since I was a tweaking bundle of nerves and had no interest in asking random strangers for directions that I would surely forget as instantaneously as they were given to me.

Whoever he was, I tapped Jackson Zapf's address into the TomTom GPS unit so I could find out for myself. It wasn't long before some lady with a proper British accent directed me onto I-95 North. After one exit she had me making arbitrary lefts and illogical rights and it wasn't long before she lost all patience and began to scold me for missing a turn. She quickly recalculated my dwindling options and ultimately decided to punish me by directing me through the bowels of Stamford, a neighborhood that good Greenwich boys had no other reason to visit beside scoring drugs. I knew the place like the back of my hand.

It wasn't long before Lady TomTom exclaimed jubilantly, 'You have reached your destination!' Her electronic exuberance made me feel like we'd arrived at Buckingham Palace, yet the non-descript, beige stucco house on the corner seemed more like the borough of Queens than anywhere Queen Elizabeth would reside, let alone visit. The fact that it was located next door to a Catholic Church did nothing but put me on edge, so after parking on the street I rewarded myself with a small bump off my key.

THINGS WERE BECOMING HAZY and I was increasingly panicked about turning the engine off, just in case the battery hadn't fully charged. Time was confusing and I had no idea how long the car had been running since it had been jumped. I remember feeling a bit uneasy when I got out because there was this suspicious looking group of white suburban teenagers who longed to be black urbanites. They smoked Newports and wore

Tommy Hilfiger jeans that were so baggy that the collective group could have easily fit into a single pair.

I was paranoid about leaving the car because it was the only thing in my rapidly diminishing world that I cared about. It was something tangible that represented Daddy, whoever he turned out to be. I spent an inordinate amount of time figuring out how to simultaneously lock the doors with no convertible top and a running engine that would continue to charge the battery, but ultimately couldn't figure out the puzzle but locked the doors just in case. Since I needed an insurance policy, specifically protecting me from theft, I caught the attention of the tween-aged hoodlums by producing a wad of twenties from my wallet. They stared at me in disbelief as I ripped the bills in half, symmetrically bisecting each and every one of Andrew Jackson's faces. Some lanky white kid with corn rows called me a 'Dumb-ass, Crackhead!'

I handed the left half of President Jackson's profiles to the kid who had braids like an albino Snoop Dogg and said, 'If you guys make sure nothing happens to the car, then this dumb-ass Crackhead will come back and give you the other halves. Deal?'

'That depend, Mister,' said a less trustful blonde boy with an affected Ebonics accent, 'How long you be?'

I said, 'If you've got somewhere else to go, don't let me hold you up.' I walked away as one of them started to whisper that I was that faggot from *The Big Brother,* 'Not the one with the missing leg you fucking idiot. The fag who lost *The Big Brother.*'

I walked down the path toward Jackson Zapf's house and wondered if I would have preferred growing up next to a church rather than a graveyard. I looked up at the windows on the second floor and wondered which bedroom would have been ours?

I held my breath and pressed the doorbell which chimed as if it were a twelve-inch extended dance remix. When the door finally opened I was nervous about making eye contact with the heavyset middle-aged woman who peered through the screen door at me. A shiver sent goose pimples down my arms when she opened the door.

She said, 'Hello?' cautiously, but I was too timid to meet her eyes, let alone respond. 'Can I help you?' she asked while taking a very long drag from an even longer cigarette. I stammered, sweating as she exhaled through the screen and informed me nonchalantly, 'The A.A. meeting is next door in the church basement.'

I looked up at her, shamefully, as we locked eyes and examined each other much too eagerly for supposed strangers. At first I was convinced she knew I was tweaking, but then wondered if the man listed on my birth certificate was actually our biological father then she might just be bugging out on my uncanny resemblance to Jackson Zapf? Suddenly I got all paranoid and felt like I should avert my eyes before she could put two and two together, except by that point I couldn't look away.

She was actually very beautiful despite the fact that she was wearing way too much makeup, kind of like a mob-wife character on *The Sopranos*. Everything about her was impeccable, as if she'd spent the last eight hours doing her hair, makeup and dangerously long nails, on the off chance that some long lost, tweaking reality TV star might ring her double-stanza doorbell and tell her they might be related.

WHEN I ATTEMPTED to speak it was as if I had laryngitis. Although my lips moved, my voice was M.I.A. I cleared my throat and sounded like a pack-a-day smoker of non-filters, obviously I needed to give the pipe a rest. I tried not to feel guilty about my pleasures as I asked, 'Is Jackson Zapf here?'

Mrs. Soprano was still chomping on her sugarless Nicorette cud when she bellowed, 'Oh. My. *Gawd!*' as if she was having a heart attack. 'You're the boy from the *teavy!*'

I felt like an idiot and stared down at my Nikes until she unlocked the screen door and began to gush, 'Did Father Jack win some contest, or what?' Her words were accented with various pops and gum clicks as if she were a bushman from the Australian outback, speaking in her native click-click-bubble-gum-tongue.

'You could say that,' I chuckled nervously, while assuming that my unwelcomed presence would likely make ol' Jack feel more like he'd lost a contest. Then I was confused as to why Mrs. Soprano had called him father because when I looked closely she seemed much too old to be Jackson's daughter, let alone our half-sister, or step-sister, but I wasn't about to get into all that with her.

'Is he around?'

'Father Jack is actually giving a special afternoon Mass right now. With everything going on in this crazy world we live in we had to add an extra masses. Did you know anyone from the Towers?'

I shook my head while taking note of a substantially large cross hanging amongst random religious paraphernalia and realized that Daddy did not live in a house, he lived in a rectory. And that's when it became immediately obvious why Father Daddy had hung up the phone. He didn't want anything to do with us because a Priest with twins might raise a few eyebrows.

'You can probably still catch the end of his homily. Or you're welcome to wait here in the rectory. He always checks in with me after Mass.'

'I'll catch the homily,' I said, surprised by my choice since I hadn't been to church since Moya stopped dragging us, mostly because we would giggle through the whole mass, probably because we were always stoned.

'Sure, honey. But before you go, would it be okay if I got an autograph? It's not every day a *teavy* star comes knocking on the door at St. Clement's.'

I reached into my pocket and pulled out what felt like a thick pen, but in reality turned out to be a charred meth pipe. We both shared an awkward giggle as her eyes darted toward the A.A. meeting.

Mrs. Soprano ordered me to, 'Stay right there!' as she ran back into the rectory and returned with a Sharpie and a bible to write on. I signed my name with the permanent marker and shrugged when I noticed that my shaky signature had bled through the paper, permanently marking her missal. She noticed too and giggled as I handed it back to her, 'Don't worry about it, honey. We're lousy with bibles around here.'

I WALKED INTO the A-framed, brick-faced church, which, much like me, felt completely out of place in the neighborhood. A quick bump off my key in the empty vestibule gave me the confidence to burst through the second set of double doors as if I were Dustin Hoffman, attempting to speak his peace at the end of *The Graduate*.[38]

A few Holy Rollers turned around and immediately passed judgment by giving me the evil eye, but I didn't let it faze me even though I was starting to feel a bit paranoid. Like a magnet, I was drawn toward the man standing at the

---

[38] *The Graduate* is a 1967 American comedy-drama film starring Dustin Hoffman as a recent college grad who is seduced by an older woman, Mrs. Robinson (Anne Bancroft), and then proceeds to fall in love with her daughter. Things get a bit messy when the daughter leaves her fiancé at the altar and escapes the chapel with Hoffman, trapping the attendees inside.

pulpit on the altar. My goose pimples re-emerged as I moved closer, slowly down the aisle, like a blushing bride. I was completely mesmerized by Father Daddy's face as I walked toward the altar, toward the voice that didn't sound like ours, toward the priest who didn't look anything like I remembered, toward the Father who may or may not have been our father.

Father Daddy stopped what he was doing mid-homily, glaring at his mid-Mass intruder almost as intensely as I was memorizing him. My eyes poured over every line in his aging face, looking for recognition as if I were watching an episode of *America's Most Wanted*. Time had not been kind to the man who left his family to take a vow of poverty and live life with minimal moisturizer.

I recognized a familiar kindness in his eyes when he paused his homily to stare at me with a curiousness as if he were trying to place my face.

Eventually he continued, 'We're still hoping we'll wake up. We're still hoping we'll open our sleepy eyes and think, What a horrible dream!' he paused for dramatic effect before his voice returned in a much softer tone, 'But we won't. What we saw was not a dream. Planes did gouge towers. Flames did consume our fortress. People did perish. It was no dream and, dear Father, we are sad.'

I couldn't help but look around at the parishioners' faces scattered about me. I saw emotions I'd never seen expressed before. Their expressions were lost and their collective sentiment felt completely foreign, which probably would have had a sobering effect if I hadn't been so damn high.

'We are sad, Father, for as the innocent are buried, our innocence is buried as well. We thought we were safe. Perhaps we should have known better. But we didn't know that the entire world could change in an instant. And so we come to you. We don't ask you for help; we beg you for it.

And so we thank you for these hours of prayer. The Enemy sought to bring us to our knees. He had no idea, however, that we would kneel before you. And he has no idea what you can do. We thank you, dear Father, for these hours of unity. Americans are praying as one.' The congregation responded on auto-pilot with a collectively somber, 'Amen.'

I'm sure you would refer to me as a narcissistic asshole, but while I was listening to Father Daddy's words I felt as if he were speaking to me directly. I was sad and he was my father. Our father. I had come to him for help, to beg him for it, on my knees if need be. And I decided right then and there, mostly because of his inspiring sermon, that I would not take his 'no' for an answer.

HAD I BEEN SOBER, I never would have risen for communion, but at the time I couldn't pass up any opportunity to get a closer look at the non-celibate priest who, according to Mommie Dearest, may or may not have been responsible for our DNA.

However, the closer I got, the further the odds of a biological connection became. I stood directly in front of him, studying him, when Father Daddy offered me the Host and said, 'Body of Christ.'

Instead of holding out my hands or opening my mouth in acceptance of the sacrament, I stared deeply into his blue eyes. Time ground to a halt as I inspected each and every crevice of his face for further recognition. It was as if I were privately scouring over my own pores in one of those concave make-up mirrors that contort reflections.

With each awkward moment that passed, Father Daddy became a less and less likely candidate to be our biological father. Nothing about his face reminded me of ours. His baby blues were too squinty, almost as if he were part Asian, whereas our hazel eyes gave us a more rounded, all-American look. His complexion seemed ruddy in a red-head-ish, 'Get me out of the sun' kind of way, even though what was left of his hair had long ago turned grey. His chin was slightly recessed, almost as if it were playing hide-and-go-seek beneath his overbite.

It was rather short but the communion line ground to a halt behind me since I neither opened my mouth nor extended my palms to accept the Styrofoam wafer of Christ. Father Daddy smiled awkwardly, confused by my hesitance, and that's when I undeniably remembered him even though Mommie Dearest had thrown out every last photo of him.

The feeling must have been mutual because, even after his eighteen year hiatus, Father Daddy's expression quickly turned inanimate, as if he had seen a ghost. When I said, 'I think I'm your son,' his already pale cheeks appeared to bleach before my eyes, practically matching his priestly collar.

Our rapid breath filled the stillness of the Church with anticipation until I realized that Father Daddy's kind eyes had definitely left the building. His formerly friendly expression had quickly been replaced with lament. Kind of like how Adam must've looked after Eve confessed to feasting upon the forbidden fruit. He wiped his forehead free of perspiration and guiltily glanced around the church like a nervous shoplifter scanning for security cameras. Then he said, 'This is extremely inappropriate.' We were at a standstill. For the first time I sensed that he was scared. Of me, no less. Or possibly you.

Our Communion standstill ultimately frustrated one of the brutish Altar Girls who had been holding her gold plated tray beneath my chin the entire time. Flustered by the expanding line that had formed behind me, her freckled face finally blurted out, 'Eat it!' I did as I was told and stuck out my tongue at Father Daddy who quickly shoved the host into my mouth and shuffled me aside to welcome his next parishioner.

I left the church in silence, grinding on the Styrofoam wafer of Christ while pondering, possibly aloud, about the last time I had actually chewed on something besides the enamel of my own teeth.

I SAT ON THE STOOP of St. Clement's, nervously picking the sores on my face as I hid beneath an architectural eave from a large black raven perched upon a telephone pole. The bird gave me a lengthy, ominous look until the brutish Altar Girl swung open the Church doors. Father Daddy and his anemic congregation emerged, and after an initial glare he blatantly ignored me while shaking hands with his parishioners.

Father Daddy offered them kind words and promised to pray for missing loved ones while secretly wishing that I had been amongst the casualties. Some of the parishioners must have noticed his disdain because they began to look at me funny. I'm not exactly sure what they were saying, but it was hard not to miss their disparaging whispers as I sat there quietly, patiently, enduring their mockery while obsessively chewing my fingernails.

That's when, out of the corner of my eye I noticed the raven dive bomb me from the telephone pole as if it had followed me all the way from the *Wall Street Widows* set. I wondered aloud, 'What are the odds?' as I leapt out of its path and tripped down four, possibly six stairs before ducking for cover. I landed in a puddle of gasping Catholics who seemed more alarmed by my presence than by the bloodthirsty raven.

I began to laugh. Awkwardly. Nobody knew exactly how to react. They all kind of looked up to Father Daddy for guidance, but he was too busy pretending nothing unusual had happened, even though my face was nestled comfortably between his pair of sensible, rubber-soled shoes.

The good news was that Father Daddy was finally forced to acknowledge my presence. He had no choice but to deal with the situation, a.k.a. me, as he reluctantly offered me his hand, mostly to save face amongst his devoted flock who had practically begun to pray for my salvation. Father Daddy's hairy forearm lifted me from his holy sidewalk a tad too forcefully and I began to say, 'Thanks,' but Father Daddy's helpful gesture quickly segued into a punishing heave as he excused himself from his flock and began to yank me away from the curious congregation of Catholics.

He said something like, 'Let's take a little walk, shall we?' as if I would soon be sleeping with the fishes. I stumbled as Father Daddy shoved me down the neglected sidewalk and barked, 'Who told you could come here?' in an entitled tone that sounded more *90210* Jason Priestly[39] than Catholic Priestly.

Luckily the car was still being guarded by my pasty suburban Homies who quickly surmised that the other halves of their Andrew Jacksons might be in jeopardy. They began to surround us which had a confounding effect on Father Daddy. He said, 'Excuse us?' in the form of a question.

---

[39] Jason Priestley is a Canadian-American actor best known as the virtuous Brandon Walsh on the television series *Beverly Hills, 90210*. A bit cocky and self-assured, he singlehandedly brought back sideburns back into fashion in the early 1990s.

'You okay?' Snoop Pupp asked me. I nodded and requested his aid in helping Father Daddy get into the car, to which he and his homies happily obliged.

I opened the passenger door and my circle of thugs began to tighten their already tight circle around Father Daddy until he had no other choice but to get in. He asked, 'Is this my old Porsche? What happened to the top?' as I moved the pile of galvanized steel chain onto the back seat so he could sit more comfortably.

'Why didn't you take it with you?'

'Because it was in your mother's name so she chained it to a tree. Everything was in her name. I walked away from the marriage with nothing.'

I slammed the door and handed over Andrew Jackson's better halves to Snoop Pupp while his posse kept an eye on Father Daddy like prison guards.

Snoop Pupp said, 'Dude, I'd ask for an autograph, but I don't want my girlfriend to think I'm a fag.'

'And I'd sign one but I wouldn't want your girlfriend to think I was straight,' I winked. The Homeboys shared a homophobic, 'No he didn't!' as Snoop Pupp raised his fist slowly and held it up in the air, apparently for me to tap.

When I got in the driver's seat Father Daddy couldn't even look at me, 'You know, I am breaking the law just by being here with you.'

Although I was good at breaking laws, I attempted to break the ice with a smile, 'I won't tell if you won't,' but Father Daddy's frosty demeanor continued to stare out the window, obviously plotting an escape.

'You shouldn't have come here,' he said, finally turning to look at me, obviously sickened by what he saw.

'Daddy, all this time I thought you were dead.'

He lost his temper momentarily, 'Don't call me that!' but quickly regained his composure, 'I am not your father.'

'But you're the only father I've ever known. She told us you died in The Accident.'

He shook his head, 'Your mother. I don't know what to tell you.'

'My mother is a very sick woman.'

'So you know?' his demeanor suddenly changed, trading in his disgust for pity.

'Know what?'

'Who your real father is?'

'Until this afternoon I assumed you were my real father. My real dead father.'

'Listen Thom, I'm very sorry for abandoning you with her but you've got to understand that it wasn't my choice. As you know your grandfather was a very powerful man and he slapped me with a gag order after the settlement.'

'Actually, I know nothing about my grandfather. I never met him or anyone else in my family. Besides Tim. And now you.'

'Your Grandfather wasn't a bad man. He was just trying to protect his family. More or less.'

'What did you do?'

Father Daddy chuckled, 'Ha! What did I do? That's an excellent question, Thom! And one that I am legally bound not to answer. Even if I were free to tell you what happened, I wouldn't. Some things are better left unsaid.'

I was completely enraptured by the secrets surrounding our past and had trouble processing the fact that it was probably even more checkered than I had suspected. I kept asking questions, 'So who is Thom Thompson, Junior?'

'He's your Uncle. And he's a very bad man.'

'Why would she name me after my Uncle?'

'I don't understand. Your name isn't Thom Zapf?'

I shook my head, 'Thom Thompson. The third.'

I reached into my pocket and produced my birth certificate where it clearly stated my name was Thompson

Thompson III. Incredulous, Father Daddy grabbed the document, 'This doesn't make any sense.' He scoured the birth certificate until he realized that it had been changed. He pointed out the amendment date and said, 'Is your mother so twisted that she actually changed your name? Wow. Just wow.'

'Try growing up with her.' Father Daddy chuckled at my joke and it made me feel closer to him, as if we were both veterans from the same unwinnable war. That's when I asked, 'Why did you become a priest?'

'Actually that was always my master plan. The better question is, Why did I get married? I met your mother while I was in divinity school. They encouraged us to experiment and sow our wild oats before taking a vow of celibacy. And to make a long story short, I experimented.'

'That's crazy.'

'Perhaps. Yet somehow not quite as crazy as lying to a future priest that he was the father of your unborn child.'

'Why would she do that?'

'And that's how we come full-circle back to the gag order.'

'You really can't tell me *anything?*'

'Can't. And won't.'

I **FLINCHED** when Father Daddy awkwardly reached out and pulled my limp body toward him. My initial surprise was quickly replaced by confusion, then ultimately by distrust as I tried to push him away. My body started to convulse uncontrollably as emotional toxins began their long overdue and completely unexpected release. Twenty-one years of pent up frustration began to seep out of me, mostly in the form of tears.

I grabbed onto Father Daddy's black priestly frock as if I were a baby, his baby, holding on as tightly as I possibly could, partly because I was scared to let go of him, but mostly because I was more worried that he'd let go of me and disappear again. And when that moment finally arrived, and Father Daddy attempted to pull away from our embrace, I felt an instant uneasiness until his recently freed hand returned to stroke my hair. It felt so good, so primal, so paternal that my sobbing began its emotional crescendo, becoming more and more uncontrollable to the point where I began to convulse, almost epileptically.

I hyperventilated and buried my tears deep into his comforting shoulder as he whispered repeatedly into my ear, "Shhh. Everything's gonna be okay," and for some unknown reason, against all odds, I found myself wanting to believe him. Needing to. It had been so long since everything had been okay. Since anything had been okay.

There I was. Red faced and puffy eyed. Sitting next to the man who used to be our Daddy, yet not our father. Ironically he was everyone's Father with a capital F. Or at least every Catholic's Father. Anyway.

FATHER DADDY BROKE the silence as my tears began to wane, 'I'm so sorry. I know how hard all this is for you because I had to put it all behind me years ago.'

Since I wasn't quite sure if I fully trusted him and definitely wasn't sure what my next move should be, I ended up staring at him in this weird, slightly unsettling, yet intensely passionate sort of way as my mind raced through my dwindling options.

'Will you help me, Daddy?'

4

ALTHOUGH MY GRANDPARENTS
had legally bound their ex-son-in-law to keep his mouth
shut and have no contact with his twins until we were
twenty-one, they hadn't banned him from navigating me to
their house. I tried to ignore the ominous helicopter,
mostly so I wouldn't draw attention or upset Father
Daddy, but it had basically been tailgating us during our
entire trek through Greenwich. I decided it had to have
something to do with the terrorist attacks. That it had to.

I'm not sure if I was just being paranoid but I popped a
couple Xanax just in case, and when Father Daddy asked, I
told him they were Tic-Tacs. I was completely on edge as
he tried to impress me about how the Thompsons lived on
a private island in the most exclusive private gated
community in all of Greenwich. Ironically the only thing
that made any real impression was how obsessed Father
Daddy and his vow of poverty were with copious amounts
of decrepitly old money. He wrongly assumed that I would
be, too, so I tried to assuage his fears by assuring him that
big houses didn't intimidate me. After all, I grew up in
Greenwich and, until recently, lived in Beverly Hills.

Father Daddy actually guffawed at my comparison. 'You
might as well have grown up in The South Bronx
compared to where I'm taking you.' It didn't really matter
what Father Daddy thought as long as he was helping, so I
humored him by letting him play Henry Higgins,[40]

---

[40] *My Fair Lady* is a movie musical depicting a misogynistic and arrogant
phonetics professor, Henry Higgins, as he wagers that he can take flower girl
Eliza Doolittle (Audrey Hepburn) and turn her Cockney accent into a proper
English one, thereby making her presentable in high society. The best part is

coaching me on what to say, how to say it, and when to say it just in case my (allegedly) ridiculously wealthy family deemed me worthy enough of meeting them. As we drove past Greenwich High School I wondered if Father Daddy might want to make a pit stop in the parking lot so he could work on my elocution and teach me the art of a proper curtsy.

IRONCIALLY, as we approached the Indian Harbor neighborhood security gate, my inner Eliza Doolittle[41] began to surface. I felt increasingly panicked as we drove past stately mansions that had been ostentatiously built several generations before the current occupants' money had officially turned old.

The security gate felt nothing like Universal Studios where the Guard would have waved us in merely because we were white people driving a Porsche, albeit one tweaked out white guy driving a Porsche with a decapitated convertible top. When I stopped at the Indian Harbor security gate it felt like we'd been stopped by the Gestapo. The guard grilled us for names, ranks and serial numbers, not to mention the reason behind our unannounced visit.

'The Thompsons aren't expecting anyone,' he said, studying his clipboard, studying me, 'Otherwise I'd have you on my list.'

'We tried to call, but my cell died,' I held up my phone for show.

Father Daddy smiled, 'It's a bit of a spontaneous visit.'

'Who should I say is calling?'

---

that Audrey Hepburn's singing voice is dubbed by a proper English one.
[41] Did you already forget the vital information you just learned from the last footnote?

I looked at Father Daddy for guidance and he said, 'Go ahead. Tell them who you are.'

'It's Thom Thompson.'

After hearing my name the Indian Harbor SS guard started singing a different tune, 'Are you Mr. Thompson's grandson? I mean, the late Mr. Thompson?'

I gave a nervous smile before the guard called the Thompsons. Our family. Whoever answered his call was obviously so surprised by our visit that she insisted on speaking directly to me. I tried to pass off the task to Father Daddy but he just shrugged, 'Trust me. If I get on that phone we'll never get in. And do not mention that I'm the one who brought you.'

I stepped out of the Porsche, took the phone from the guard and offered a tentative, 'Hello.'

'Who is this?' demanded a husky female voice.

'Thom Thompson.'

'My father passed away and my brother doesn't have any children. What kind of sick joke is this?'

'I'm Thom Thompson the third. My mother is Prudence Thompson.'

'That's impossible. The twins died in a horrific accident twenty years ago. Besides they were Zapf's, not Thompson's.'

'I have no idea why everybody thinks we're dead, but I can assure you we're both very much alive.' Father Jack gave me a confused look which let me know that he was also under the assumption that you were dead but I didn't have time to justify your existence as I was busy justifying my own. 'Apparently my mother had all our names legally changed to Thompson before I was even conscious that I had a last name.'

Then there was a pause so pregnant that I could have planned and thrown a baby shower before she responded, 'Put the guard back on.'

I'm not sure what she spoke about with the guard but I felt like my heart might pound right out of my chest during their lengthy conversation. It didn't help matters that he kept looking down at me, suspiciously, over his shoulder. Luckily, nobody seemed to pay much attention to the helicopter, probably because it was camouflaged by the mature Maple trees that lined the roads of the entire private neighborhood. Regardless, it was hovering at an altitude low enough to make the leaves quiver above us, and me quiver beneath it.

After the guard got off the phone he raised the gate and, somewhat reluctantly, granted us admission to his lush kingdom. Father Daddy directed me through the gated neighborhood, which, now that we had passed the Gestapo, felt neither more exclusive nor gargantuan than others I had visited before. That is until we turned onto Raven's Neck Island Causeway and I saw the house. Or, more specifically, didn't see the house. The private island was so extensive that the house was not actually visible to the naked eye from the mainland. An ominous shiver shook my already jittery body as I approached another gate, this one gilded, at the end of an extensive causeway which doubled as the private island's driveway.

'They call it Raven's Nest Island because the hilly terrain looks like the nest of a Raven,' Father Daddy said. 'It's the only privately owned island in the entire town of Greenwich,' but I already knew this because the famous piece of property was beyond legendary. The fact that its mysterious owners were relatives of mine was beyond comprehension, or would have been had I not been suffering from an exceptionally crippling case of déjà vu. I reached out the driver's side window and pressed the intercom call button to dial the unseen house which I somehow already knew was located on the south side of the island compound, across from the manicured grounds, beyond the unseen tennis court.

My heart pounded but ultimately sank to a grinding halt when a hollow, 'Hello?' echoed over the brass plated intercom system. I stammered as if I were in the middle of a scene and had forgotten my next line, hoping Father Daddy would eventually yell, 'Cut!' But I became even more intimidated when the tinny voice repeated herself, this time a bit more surly, *'Hello?'*

Father Daddy nudged me until I leaned over and cleared my voice into the brass intercom, 'It's Thom again. We're at the gate now.'

She asked, 'Who's we?' as Father Daddy elbowed me. 'Is your brother Tim with you, too?'

'Um, no. It's just me. I guess I was just using the royal *we.*'

Father Daddy began to brief me about our Aunt and I remember wondering what kind of cruel mother would nickname her daughter Pudge as the polished double gates began to open. Neither of us spoke as I drove across the manmade causeway that connected Raven's Nest Island to the mainland of Greenwich, winding past private horse stables and an impeccable Har Tru tennis court until we had a straight shot through the lengthy, meticulously manicured, tree-lined drive. I drove slower than I realized was possible, probably because I was wary of the next wave of déjà vu that I knew would be waiting for me when I reached the driveway's end. I parked in the circular cobblestone turnabout which featured an unassuming fountain in the grassy center.

Everything was impressively understated and surprisingly unpretentious. Somehow the house fit into its grand surroundings even though a home half its size would have felt like a ridiculous, over-the-top parody in Beverly Hills. I was so out of my comfort zone that I completely forgot about the charging battery and ended up turning the engine off, but was immediately soothed by the rippling water in Indian Harbor when the purr of the engine cut off. I sat silently for a moment which must have appeared like I was waiting for a Bell Hop at the Ritz Carlton to help us check-in, but in reality I was just listening for low-lying aircraft. When the coast was clear I stepped out of the car but Father Daddy just sat there.

'Aren't you coming?'

'Absolutely not. I shouldn't have come this far. If I go in that house with you then we'll both get kicked out before you find out what you're looking for.'

I WALKED AMBIVALENTLY toward the grand vestibule that framed the gated glass entry and realized the door was most likely made of crystal, which, of course, did nothing but made my body crave another quick hit of confidence. Since my paranoia was already on high alert, I knew it would be catastrophic for me to be totally tweaking in that kind of environment, but by the time I rang the eloquent doorbell I had nothing but crystal on my mind.

After a few uncomfortable moments I was greeted by a white-uniformed, blonde woman who appeared more pinched than Nurse Ratched from *One Flew Over the Cuckoo's Nest*. She inspected me carefully before allowing me to enter, quickly informing me that both Miss and Mrs. Thompson were expecting me in the study. Without further ado Nurse Wretched did an abrupt about-face and began to walk away from me with every expectation that I would follow.

Once inside, the palatial house felt as cozy as the winter Icehotel in Sweden, and the décor was equally as frigid.

The sheer scale of everything made me feel miniscule, practically insignificant as I followed my guide across several, massive Persian rugs, each creating different seating areas in the colossal lobby—I mean living room. The views through the beveled glass windows were nothing short of spectacular. I was mesmerized by sailboats moored in Greenwich Harbor, rocking back and forth in the shimmering water of the Long Island Sound just beyond the island's ridiculously long private pier. That's when I noticed the boathouse situated at the far end of the dock. It began to beckon me in a way that I knew it had long ago when you and I had gleefully raced each other all the way to the end and back.

Far off in the distance I noticed the familiar New York skyline. Only like most things in my life, it wasn't at all familiar anymore. Instead of the city being bookended between the Empire State and the Twin Towers, it now appeared lopsided. Although enormous thick clouds of billowing white smoke were still visible from thirty miles away, the city's balance was so off that it seemed as if midtown might begin to sway off kilter and plunge into the sea.

It was so thoroughly disconcerting that I turned away from the window and held on tightly to the thick fabric curtain while I did my breathing exercises. I hadn't realized I'd abandoned my escort until Nurse Wretched called after me, obviously frustrated by my slow place and attention deficit. I hurried down the long hallway, overflowing with museum quality pieces. One painting was disturbingly familiar, although I'm still not sure if I was remembering it from an art history class I failed just before getting thrown out of Bennington? Or if I remembered it from hanging on the exact same wall the last time I visited? I think it was a Monet. Possibly a Manet. Although it was familiar, I still failed the class.

NURSE WRETCHED abruptly gestured for me to halt as she stopped in front of a set of enormous mahogany sliding doors, tapping lightly to announce my previously unannounced arrival. One of the doors jerked open almost instantaneously, but only about two inches. I gasped when a terrifyingly old woman stuck one of her wrinkly, bloodshot eyes through the slight gap. And as if that wasn't enough of a deterrent, she upped the ante by screaming violently through the sliver of the door jam, 'Go away!'

I was rendered speechless, not to mention completely disturbed by the old woman's running nose, while she looked at me suspiciously through the crack and asked, more like demanded, 'What is Skipper doing here!' only not at all in the form of a question. Her initial look of a recognition quickly morphed into utter disgust. Then she turned to Nurse Ratched and scolded her, 'I'm sure no one informed you, but Skipper is no longer welcome at Raven's Nest.' She was feisty and had the familiar accent of a Kennedy, or possibly Katherine Hepburn—before the tremor.

THE ELDERLY WOMAN slithered into the shadows after Nurse Wretched opened the sliding doors and allowed me entry into the wood-paneled library. She spoke softly but firmly to the frightened yet equally frightening old woman who was dressed impeccably, as if she were still a lady who lunched even though her nose was running down her face like a toddler. She had obviously lost her mind long ago.

Nurse Wretched reminded her patroness, 'Mrs. Thompson, this is not Skipper. I would never disobey you and allow Skipper into Raven's Nest.' The confused old woman peered at me distrustfully, then scurried away and disappeared into one of a pair of matching oversized brown leather Chesterfields. The iconic chairs were placed in front of a fireplace so massive that most New Yorkers would have been thrilled to partition it and illegally sublet the substantial area beyond the mantle.

I kept rubbernecking the spry old woman as if she were a car accident, watching her head pop up and down periodically from behind her enormous chair, almost like an antique Whack-a-Mole in a vain attempt to keep tabs on her Raven's Nest infiltrators.

Nurse Wretched walked away from me in order to calm her elderly patient as a disembodied voice called me over from a dark corner on the opposite side of the windowless, mahogany-paneled library, 'Thom?' After my eyes adjusted to the dim lighting, I attempted to contain my shock when I got my first look at her.

'Don't be scared of your old Aunt. I'm just fat,' she said, literally referencing the enormous elephant in the room in such a way that was meant to put me at ease.

'Come over here and let me get a look at you,' Aunt Pudge cackled from behind an *US Weekly*. She was lying on a queen size bed, which seemed oddly out of place in the library until I realized the double doored library entrance was probably the only one suitable for her to fit through. The large bed appeared almost twin-sized since Aunt Pudge covered every square inch as if she were an over-stuffed duvet. At first glance her nickname seemed like cruel and unusual punishment, but as I got closer I realized that she was so shockingly obese that it was actually quite complimentary. She would need to go on the Atkins Diet just to walk through the door jamb, an activity which, from the looks of her, hadn't happened in years.

My morose thoughts began to wonder how a regular sized toilet could support her body? Then I realized that the likelihood of her getting out of her bed, let alone squeezing through a bathroom door, was next to nil. Just like Charlie's grandparents in *Willy Wonka* Aunt Pudge was forever trapped in her bed, except for the fact that there wasn't any extra room on her mattress for any other grandparents, as there was barely enough space for her everlasting supply of Gobstoppers and Wonka Bars that were scattered around her comforter, to comfort her.[42]

I wondered what it would feel like to never leave my bed? My thoughts obviously turned to Mommie Dearest's agoraphobia about leaving the house, but to be confined to one spot, one position. I'm not sure how long I was standing there, tweaking out on Aunt Pudge's situation before she waved me over with a brief flick of her thick wrist. It had probably been the extent of her exercise for the week.

Her jaw dropped incrementally as I inched my way over. She said, 'With that chin there's no question you're a Thompson.' However as hard as I tried I was unable to locate any resemblance to Aunt Pudge's own chin as it appeared to be nothing more than a nasty mosquito bite, a red bump that protruded through the folds of her missing neck.

She said, 'Mother, come say hello to your grandson, Thom.' But our senile old Grammy shook her head mistrustfully and muttered something to herself about how wayward children could ruin an entire family's reputation. From there she somehow segued into a story about how

---

[42] *Willy Wonka & the Chocolate Factory* is a 1971 musical film adaptation of the 1964 novel *Charlie and the Chocolate Factory* by Roald Dahl. The film tells the story of Charlie as he receives a golden ticket and visits Willy Wonka's chocolate factory with four other nasty children from around the world. All four of Charlie's grandparents share one bed, and no, it isn't an orgy. It's a fourgy.

her teeth were made of wood, just like George Washington. At the time it seemed to make perfect sense.

Aunt Pudge rolled her eyes and spoke in a whisper, 'You'll have to excuse my mother. Or rather your grandmother. She's been suffering from Alzheimer's for years. It's difficult to watch her drift in and out, but today's actually been a good day.' With that she pulled a cookie from a jar resting atop a pile of magazines on her nightstand and popped it into her mouth as if she were rewarding a puppy.

Aunt Pudge gobbled it down before her attention slowly waned away from her taste buds and she began to squint at me. It was a bit disconcerting since it gave off the illusion that her eyes had literally been swallowed into her enormous head. 'I can't get over how much you look like my brother when he was your age.'

'He looks like Skipper because he is Skipper!' exclaimed Grammy, peeking from behind her chair as if she were one of those crotchety, old Muppets on the balcony.

'Who's Skipper?' I asked.

'You're Skipper! And you're not welcome here!' Grammy screamed with intense fear. However far gone she was it was obvious that she hated Skipper. And in turn, hated me.

Aunt Pudge explained patiently, 'For the last time, Mother, this is not Skipper. This is Thom. He's one of Bunny's twins that you said died in The Accident. But here he is! Living proof. Your grandson is all grown up.'

I attempted to smile, but what I ended up expressing was probably more like the pained look on Grammy's face as she tried to process all the information in her deteriorating brain.

'The twins are dead!' Grammy screamed defiantly and became visibly upset. 'Skipper is dead! Your father is dead! Everybody is dead but me. Why am I still here?'

'Mother, stop talking such morbid things. And just because you and Daddy cut Skipper off decades ago does not make him dead.'

Grammy's only response was, 'He's dead to me!'

Aunt Pudge rolled her eyes and whispered, 'Mother's mind might be shot but her hearing's still 20/20.'

'Mother,' Pudge said calmly, 'It's time for your stories. *As the World Turns* is about to start any minute.'

Grammy's demeanor changed as instantaneously as a toddler's, 'Really?' Like a child being bribed away with candy, she did the emotional equivalent of a 180° before doing the physical equivalent by disappearing down long the hall.

The rolls between Aunt Pudge's elbow and her shoulder made a flapping gesture for me to sit in the chair next to her bed as she muted CNN with her remote. Explosive imagery of the World Trade Center continued to echo through the hushed room, 'I'm sorry but I can't bring myself to turn it off. It's just so upsetting. All those innocent people did nothing more threatening than go to work.'

My attention briefly segued to the upsetting footage until Aunt Pudge gestured to her mother, 'I'd love to ask her why she told me you died in The Accident, but I doubt her answer would make a lick of sense.' She gave me a once over and asked, 'Did some Good Samaritan adopt you poor boys after Bunny was institutionalized?'

'Who's Bunny?'

'I'm sorry. Bunny is my sister, Prudence. Your mother.'

'You called my mother *Bunny?*'

Pudge laughed, 'Bunny, Skipper, Pudge. My parents obviously had a WASPy knack for nicknaming their kids.'

'My mother never ended up in an institution. Although there's still time so we shouldn't give up hope.'

'I don't understand. My parents told me they had her institutionalized after The Accident.'

'If only. She lives in Old Greenwich and hasn't left the house in twenty years.'

'I don't understand why my parents would make up such horrible lies?'

'And I'm not sure why my mother would lie about my father being dead, but I'm guessing it has something to do with the reason your parents lied to you.'

'Jack is alive? Was there even an accident or did they make that up too?'

'I can assure you there was an accident. My mother's car is still sitting at the bottom of the pool. And Jack is very much alive. He's the one who told me about you.' I wanted to tell her that Father Daddy was currently waiting for me in her driveway but I got worried that it might interfere with my ultimate goal of sifting through generations of my family's mysterious lies for some truth.

'Well, if nothing else you and I certainly have a lot of catching up to do.'

'So your brother is really Thom Junior?' I asked rhetorically.

'Yes, and as far as I know he's still very much alive. If only my sister had run over him this world might be a better place. Nothing about this family was ever the same after that horrible day.' Aunt Pudge bowed her head solemnly to acknowledge the event and it was obvious that she felt uncomfortable talking about in my presence, even though I was the only one of us who had actually been part of it.

I was about to begin my interrogation when Aunt Pudge shifted her massive body and her *Star* magazine fell from what vaguely appeared to be a knee. The tabloid dropped onto the floor, in front of me, at my feet. I picked it up without missing a beat but was distracted by a small photo on the cover's upper right corner with a tagline that read, 'Big Brother's Restroom Rendezvous.'

A cold sweat took over my body as I stared at the horrid picture. The expression on my face was so dire that it would have literally stopped a truck. Or a career. I knew if I opened the so-called magazine that I would find those humiliating, incriminating pictures of us, the ones from The Abbey's bathroom stall photo shoot. I needed to get rid of it before Aunt Pudge saw it and deemed me unfit for further social interaction, so I abruptly excused myself, 'Can I use your bathroom?'

Aunt Pudge stated the obvious, 'You look pale.'

I attempted a smile when I looked up from the rag's cover but the embarrassing cover photo continued to taunt me from my lap. 'I'm fine,' I lied.

AUNT PUDGE gave me detailed directions, obviously from a distant memory when she was still able to walk around freely and use bathrooms. It was so far away I could've used a map. I slithered down the hallway with that *Star* magazine rolled tightly within my white knuckled fist for ten minutes before I realized I was lost and had to ask at least two wary servants to redirect me to the aptly named *powder* room.

Although I initially planned to powder my nose, heavily, when I saw there was a window I cracked it open and took a few necessary hits on the pipe before I found the courage to flip through the magazine and locate the twincest photos. However, when I finally found the article I wasn't the least bit prepared for what I saw.

The photo must have been doctored. But when was the last time a tabloid retouched a celebrity's photo in order to make it *less* titillating? It made no sense, but there it was in print. Exactly as I remembered. *Almost.*

There I was. Backed up against the steel divider, pants around my ankles, predictably taking a hit off the pipe. Thank God they had digitally blurred my crotch, although I was sure the untouched photo had already been plastered all over the internet. It was completely obvious what we were doing. Except, of course, for the fact that we weren't the ones doing it. Although the photo was definitely of me, you were not the one bent over in the compromising position, begging to be fucked. That role was undeniably played by the Gay Fiancé.

If an A-list sex scandal happens to a D-list celebrity who's too fucked up to remember it, does it really happen?

It didn't make any sense. Did you go back to the stall and fuck the Gay Fiancé after I left? Even though the photo looked more like you then me, and even though you had a pension for pretending to be me, I realized the culprit in question was undeniably wearing my 'Fuck Me I'm Famous' t-shirt (although the word 'fuck' had also been digitally blurred). The photo was indisputably me. And I was definitely not being raped by you. Mostly because you weren't even in the photo. Even though one might think this fact should have made me feel better, in actuality it just made me feel nauseous.

Regardless, nothing was more upsetting than the article itself, which, in a nutshell, claimed that after my short stint on *Big Brother* I had used my fifteen minutes of fame to segue into a starring role on a sitcom, but the network promptly canceled the show when they learned I had been secretly moonlighting in the adult film industry, most likely to support my expensive drug habit. First I wondered if they knew how cheap crystal was, but then I tried to focus on the actual issue at hand and became concerned with the fact that everyone and their network was confusing us and our careers. It was like everybody thought that I was you. Or even worse, that you were me. I had to put a stop to it before things got even worse, even though I couldn't imagine how that would be possible.

When I couldn't look at it any longer, I ripped the page from the magazine. I thought about throwing it out but didn't want Aunt Pudge to find it, even though it would have been impossible for her to visit the bathroom let alone bend over to pull something out of the trash.

I WAS TOTALLY tweaking when I walked back into the wood paneled room and felt completely confident that, together, Aunt Pudge and I could tackle the task at hand.

'Are you sure you're okay? You seem a bit jittery.'

'Never better,' I assured her.

'Do you think your mother might visit me sometime?' she wiped a tear.

'I can ask her for you, but she truly hasn't left the house since The Accident. Maybe you could go visit her?'

Aunt Pudge chuckled, 'Sweetie, the next time I leave Raven's Nest it's going to be in a piano crate. 'Funny, isn't it? Two shut in sisters who don't talk and an estranged brother. My parents really knew how to raise a family.'

'You could call her on the phone, but be sure to call in the morning. By lunchtime she's usually pretty out of it.'

'How do you mean?'

'Let's just say she enjoys her medication.'

'Poor thing. Give me her number. I'll call tomorrow morning and cross my fingers that she won't hang up on me.'

'Why would she do that?'

'It's funny. We were the best of friends when we were little. But as we got older, things changed. I was pretty awful to your mother,' Pudge admitted.

'How?' I dug deeper, knowing full well that I might not get another chance to ask the burning questions.

'Oh honey, it's a long, sad, pathetic story that I don't want to bore you with.' Then, seemingly out of thin air, Aunt Pudge produced a soup spoon that she immediately plunged deep into a soupy tub of Ben & Jerry's on her nightstand.

'You're definitely not boring me,' was all I could say.

Aunt Pudge took another self-medicating spoonful of Cherry Garcia and closed her eyes as her thoughts disappeared deep into the recesses of her taste buds.

Besides the distant theme music from *As the World Turns,* there was complete and utter silence while I waited impatiently for Aunt Pudge's confession. She licked ice cream from her lower lip before saying, 'My brother was a horrible, evil man,' and then quickly prescribed herself another heaping dose of Ben & Jerry's.

She paused to swallow and then rested the ice cream container deep in the folds of her belly, rubbing the tub softly with her hefty thumbs as if she were holding a church hymnal while searching for the next line of her sad song.

Aunt Pudge instinctively licked her empty spoon before continuing, 'My brother and I were less than a year apart, but were always in the same grade. Irish twins they called us. We were inseparable when we were younger. Two peas in a pod. Actually all three of us were extremely close. Too close. But we didn't have much choice. Even though Bunny was three years younger, the three of us did most everything together. Bunny was obsessed with the Mickey Mouse club and she called us the Three Mousekateers. We'd always been ostracized by the other kids for being too rich. Can you imagine? Too rich for Greenwich! Living on a private island didn't help, and none of us had any friends until Skipper and I went off to boarding school. Initially I felt terrible about leaving Bunny at Raven's Nest all by herself, but I got over it as soon as I began to make friends. I thrived at Miss Porter's, but Skipper was sent to Hotchkiss and hated it. He never fit in anywhere, even after he escaped Raven's Nest. But it wasn't until we came home for the holidays that everything changed.'

She continued, 'I've never told anyone this before, but my brother abused me.' Pudge scraped the ice cream container for the last heaping spoonful of Cherry Garcia before she continued, 'I watch Oprah every day so I don't feel ashamed about it anymore. I had no control over what happened.'

She licked her lips, 'I felt awful for Skipper since he was so miserable at school. It started innocently enough. Or so I thought. We had been separated so long. Even though I knew it was wrong, the first time it actually felt good. Like I was helping Skipper in some way. After all, we were just teenagers full of hormones. Unfortunately the good feeling didn't last long and when the guilt became unbearable, I began to plead with Skipper to stop. I told him that we would both end up in hell, but Skipper didn't care. He wanted more. He threatened to tell our parents to keep me quiet. But after a month I wanted it to stop and I didn't even care about the ramifications of my father's wrath anymore. That's when Skipper pulled out his trump card. He told me if I didn't do what he wanted, that he'd go get it from Bunny. I couldn't live with that, so I continued to let Skipper have his way with me.'

Although I was riveted by Pudge's story my thoughts, obviously, turned to you. Was everybody in our fucked up family genetically disposed to rape their siblings? Perhaps that was why Mommie Dearest was so fucked up? For the first time things started to make sense, but I didn't know what else to say besides, 'I'm so sorry.'

'Don't be sorry for me, sweetie. Nobody comes out of this story unscathed. Especially me.' Aunt Pudge took a deep breath before she continued, 'After a while I began to resent Bunny and it wasn't long before I ended up hating her. By the time Bunny hit puberty I remember praying that Skipper would leave me alone and go after your her. At that point I was a selfish teenager and all I cared about was that he left me alone. But lucky me, I was the pretty one! Ha!' Pudge laughed and the whole bed shook, 'I certainly showed him.'

If something unpleasant happens on Raven's Nest Island and Aunt Pudge swallows it, does it still exist?

'It wasn't your fault. You were a victim.'

'I've been a victim my whole life. But your mother wasn't.' Then Aunt Pudge turned to me, 'Bunny wasn't even scared to confront my father when she got pregnant out of wedlock. When she wouldn't tell him who the father was my father cut her off immediately. I'm ashamed of it now, but honestly, back then I was thrilled to be rid of her. By that time Skipper had moved out and gotten married, so he wasn't bothering me anymore. And after Bunny left I had the house to myself and honestly didn't care what happened to her. I don't think she even took anything with her when she left. After a few months we heard that Bunny married a boy named Jack who had dropped out of divinity school for her but none of us were invited to the wedding, except for my brother. After she got married my father finally came around and made his peace with Bunny so, in retrospect, there were a actually few good years. She and I were never close again, but Bunny used to bring you boys to Raven's Nest after church every Sunday and you would hop out of the car and race like the wind down to the end the dock. Bunny would run after you, terrified that you might run right into the Sound when you reached the end. Everything was almost normal until The Accident. And then it all turned to shit. Excuse my French. Given the severity of what happened I never questioned why they institutionalized her.'

'Why do you think she did it?'

'I'm not sure but I don't think she wanted to kill your father. I think she meant to kill herself.'

'And her children,' I reminded her.

'Which is why I never questioned my parents when they told me she was institutionalized.'

'And why did you think we were dead?'

'Because that's what I was told! It sounds stupid now but I didn't ask too many questions back then. I heard there was a funeral but I wasn't going out much even back then. I guess that's one thing that your mother and I have in common.'

Although it felt cruel to burden Aunt Pudge with any further mention of her brother Skipper, our Uncle Thom, I desperately needed to ask her one last question, even though just thinking about asking it practically made me ill. After hearing her story I was relieved that he wasn't long for this world but I had come this far and needed to know the truth. Deserved to.

I took a big breath, 'Do you think that Skipper might have been the one who got my mother pregnant?'

'Absolutely not!' Aunt Pudge answered so emphatically that it seemed obvious she had worried about this scenario every day of her life. 'If that were the case then why on earth would she have invited that monster to her wedding? He was your father's Best Man.'

'Really? Are you sure about that?'

Aunt Pudge scooped herself another spoonful of denial and took her time swallowing before she answered,

'Positive. In their wedding photo Skipper was standing on the alter right next to Jack.'

It was hard to argue with Pudge's logic but I began to wonder who was telling the truth? A priest with twins must not be good for business but Mommie Dearest was not to be trusted about anything. Perhaps they were both lying? Or living in such denial after The Accident that they both wanted to pretend that their marriage never existed.

'I've got to get going,' I said with a burning desire to interrogate Father Daddy further.

Aunt Pudge shifted in bed, attempting to reach her nightstand as she asked me for help, 'Before you go, be a doll and open that drawer for your old Aunt, honey.' I did as I was told and she pointed out a stack of cards bound with a rubber band.

'Take those to your mother,' she said. 'I've been sending letters to the institution for years. Christmas cards, birthday cards, you name it. But they always got returned, unopened. I thought it was because she didn't want anything to do with me, but now I know it was because she was never there. I want her to know what happened. Why I was such a bad sister. Hopefully she can forgive me.'

'She'd be lucky to have someone like you in her life.'

Aunt Pudge flashed me a warm smile and I instantly recognized the family resemblance as her dimples emerged from deep within her chubby cheeks.

3

I SAT DESPONDENT in the Porsche, parked on the cobblestone drive in front of Raven's Nest while Father Daddy asked repeatedly if I was okay.

When I noticed that the helicopter had returned and was hovering over the tennis court, the frustration burst from my mouth, 'Of course I'm not okay!'

'I can't imagine what you must be feeling right now.' A pitiful look took over his face before he gave me one of those awkward, sideways car hugs and I realized he assumed that Aunt Pudge had filled me in on our family secrets. So of course I took the opportunity to make an ASS out of U and ME and began to cry on his shoulder, going along with the charade with the hope that Father Daddy would spill the beans.

'Shhh,' he soothed me. 'Let it all out.'

Unfortunately there wasn't that much to let out and quickly found myself backed into a corner. Anything I said can and would be used against me, to expose my ulterior motives, but it was a two way street. Anything Father Daddy said can and would be used against him, too.

I continued to sob, mostly out of frustration, and partly out of worry that Father Daddy was actually one of them, or at the very least, had been turned by them while I was inside. Were they all working together now? Maybe Aunt Pudge was in on it, too? I pretended to sob while keeping one dry on the copter.

He rubbed my back, 'It was a horrible thing and it never should have happened. You and your brother were just innocent victims. And so was I for that matter.'

I sniffled and decided to take a chance, 'How were you a victim?'

'They lied to me, too.'

'About what?'

'About everything. When I found out I threatened to expose them. And that's when your mother tried to kill me.'

'Did you ever go through with it? Exposing them?'

'Only to your grandparents. In return for my silence they helped me get the marriage annulled so I could go back to divinity school and continue my chosen path. I still grapple with it today, whether or not I made the right choice. It was a horribly selfish thing to do and ended up ruining the entire family. But in the end I think the truth will always set you free.'

I found his words to be especially maddening since all I asked of him from the moment we met was for the truth. I was about to call Father Daddy out on his hypocritically righteous shit when some menacing blur of a man in a dark suit and even darker sunglasses, darted across the expansive grounds and ducked behind a tree while talking into his sleeve. He was obviously in cahoots with the helicopter, conversing with the pilot, seemingly about me. I tried to convince myself that they were just your run-of-the-mill Indian Harbor security detail, but even I couldn't swallow that much denial in one mouthful.

I abruptly pulled away from Father Daddy's hug and before he had a chance ask me what was happening, I was already speeding down the causeway, away from Raven's Nest, away of Indian Harbor, away from the helicopter. We whizzed past waterfront mansions, probably too fast, definitely attracting too much attention, but I wasn't about to take chances and get caught. At that point, the only thing I knew for sure was I was going to get to the bottom of this mess, and that whoever was following me, or whoever thought they were following you, they were not going to keep me from the truth. Especially not Father Daddy.

Father Daddy scolded me as we flew past the Gestapo's security gate and raced toward the Post Road, 'Thom, slow down! You're going to cause an accident! Where are you going?'

I followed signs to I-95 as I said very calmly, 'I'm going to set you free.'

'What are you talking about?'

'You said you grapple with your decision over telling the truth, so I've decided to set you free. With the truth.'

'What are you talking about? And where are you going? I need to get back to St. Clement's.'

I gave him a taste of his own medicine and answered him with obtuse riddles, 'First I'm taking you to see the truth.'

I could tell he was getting more and more nervous. Possibly angry. Regardless he knew I was on to him because his whole demeanor changed as I slammed the gas and ran a light that was probably more pink than yellow. Father Daddy's body jerked, almost shuddered, before his patronizing attitude returned in full force, 'That's very thoughtful,' he lied, 'but I really don't think that's a good idea.' Father Daddy's words began to calmly segue into how he needed to get back to St. Clement's for five o'clock mass.

I began to wonder if I'd ever see him again, let alone if you'd ever get a chance to meet the liar who may or may not have brought us into this world. Or would he just vanish from our lives again, much like he disappeared in 1983?

'This will be quick,' I assured him.

'I wish I could, but...'

'Oh, you can. And you will.'

'No, I won't,' he said firmly. 'I am obligated to give five o'clock mass and my parishioners need me.'

'No worries,' I said as I downshifted and slammed the Porsche into a lower gear for more torque. 'I'm a fast driver.'

Father Daddy changed tactics on a dime, 'Stop this car and let me out immediately!'

My frustration quickly turned into seething anger which seeped out in the form of vocal daggers as I brought the car to an abrupt stop in the middle of the Post Road.

'Fine. Get out! But don't expect me to keep quiet about your little secret!' And with that, I pulled out my cell and dialed information. Father Daddy unfastened his seatbelt and opened his door. We were across from the old IHOP that had been oddly rebranded as a summer patio store even though it still looked like a ski chalet. A man in a suit was sitting in an unmarked car, watching everything. Reporting everything back. I had to work quickly.

Luckily his curiosity kept Father Daddy in the car long enough for the computerized operator to ask 'Toll free directory. How may I help you?'

'Hi, I need a number for *Star Magazine*.'

'I'm flattered! You think some gossip columnist is going to care about an aging Priest at St. Clement's Church?!' Father Daddy ridiculed me with a big, fake guffaw. But one thing was for damn sure, he definitely wasn't rushing off to make five o'clock mass.

The operator told me, 'I'll connect you now.'

I looked at Father Daddy and said, 'Of course *Star Magazine* isn't gonna give a shit about some stupid Priest who had twins of wedlock. But I'm guessing they might be slightly interested in a wayward TV star on a downward spiral who gives them exclusive rights to the story about reuniting with his long lost asshole father who just happens to be a Priest.' And I bet your parishioners might be a little interested, too. That's when I reached into my back pocket and pulled out the page I'd ripped from *Star Magazine*, the one where I was supposed to be fucking you, but was somehow fucking the Gay Fiancé. I shoved it in front of Father Daddy face and said, 'Congratulations. It's a TV star.'

He grabbed the article and scanned it in disbelief, 'This story cannot end up in the news. I have a gag order and will lose everything! Why would you want to ruin my life like that? Not to mention yours?' he asked, genuinely confused.

I responded redundantly, 'The truth will set you free, Daddy.'

He screamed, 'I am not even your father!'

I pulled out my birth certificate, 'According to these legal documents you are. But I'm sure Jerry Springer will insist upon a paternity test...'

He stared silently at me until the receptionist answered my call, '*Star Magazine*. How may I direct your call?'

Father Daddy began mumbling so loudly that I had to hush him in order to conduct my blackmail in peace. 'Hi. This is Thom Abel from *Big Brother* and *Wall Street Widows*. I have a very, *very* interesting story that I think *Star Magazine* might be curious about. Could you connect me to one of the editors, please?'

'One moment.' The receptionist seemed nonplussed, like she got calls like this all the time. Luckily Father Daddy didn't know that.

I told the receptionist, 'Take your time,' and smirked at Father Daddy.

'What the hell is wrong with you?' he snarled in a fearful tone before finally acquiescing, 'Fine!' He pulled his foot back in the car and slammed the passenger door. 'Hang up the phone.'

If something unpleasant happens in the Catholic church and there are no Priests or Popes to bear witness, is it still a sin?

I snapped my phone closed and continued driving toward Old Greenwich. Toward our Home-Sweet-Hovel.

FATHER DADDY SEETHED when he finally realized I was taking him home to confront Mommie Dearest. I figured if I threw those two liars into the same room they might cancel each other out and finally expose some truth. Kind of like a double negative.

'Was your life so insanely terrible and depraved that you're actually screwed up enough to blackmail a priest?'

'You don't know anything about my life,' I said nonchalantly. 'Maybe I would have grown up to be a better person had you stuck around. Then again, what kind of fucking role model would you have been? You're the one that needs to be blackmailed into telling the truth.'

'I'm not your father! What don't you understand about that?'

'Everything. But lucky for you I'm gonna give you a chance to atone for your sins.'

Father Daddy's was speechless and slack jawed as I pulled into the driveway and he saw the decrepit condition of the house. 'It doesn't get more truthful than that, now does it?'

'How could this happen?' he asked while scanning the tangle of weeds and vines that made up the front yard.

I didn't answer as Moya came running out the back door, her pantyhose scraping their way over to me as I engaged the emergency brake. She made the sign of the cross when she saw Father Daddy, 'Child, what have you gone and done?'

Father Daddy was shocked to recognize anything amongst the decay that surrounded him, 'Moya?'

'You should know better than to come here, Jack.'

'Trust me, it wasn't by choice.'

Moya looked at me, 'You best get him out of here before your mother wakes up from her afternoon nap.'

'Come on, Moya. Aren't you the least bit curious about how this might play out? My money's on Mommie Dearest. She's definitely got the home-court advantage. But then again Father Daddy isn't strung out on valium and vodka cocktails.'

'I think maybe it's best if I just go. Moya would you mind calling me a taxi?'

None of us noticed Mother creep up behind Moya, but Father Daddy jumped when he saw the knife come slashing through his peripheral vision. Unlike Neil Patrick Harris, Father Daddy jumped in a nick of time and saved his face from a good gouging. Moya grabbed hold of Mommie Dearest's wrist and squeezed until the knife fell deep into the weeds beneath her.

Father Daddy ran behind the chestnut tree for protection while Mommie Dearest screamed at me, 'Why did you bring him here? Make him go away!'

'I thought he was our father.'

She screamed at me, 'He's not! I told you he wasn't. He's the one who ruined your father. Ruined our family!'

Father Daddy cowered from behind the tree, 'Are you going to tell the poor boy who his father is? Or are you going to make me break my gag order?'

Time slowed as Mommie Dearest stared at her ex-husband in utter defeat. She had attempted to silence him twice, years ago with her car, and this time with a butcher's knife, yet the man was still standing there, breathing, or rather panting, holding on to her secret, threatening to expose her once again. The valium-induced moment extended itself long beyond my meth-induced attention span could handle, but eventually the truth began to slur its way out of Mommie Dearest's tightly pursed lips. Unfortunately everyone knew what she was going to say before she said it, including me. 'Your father's name is Thom Thompson, Junior. My brother.'

Time stopped. I remember looking at the second hand on my watch, mostly because I was terrified to risk catching someone else's eye, or rather someone else's pity as it inevitably made its way over to me. Either the second hand was not moving, or my thoughts were moving so quickly that my eyes had become unable to perceive time passing.

Time continued to stand still while Father Daddy rubbed my back and whispered something sweet, but impenetrable, before he walked down the driveway and continued down Tomac Avenue toward St. Clement's without ever looking back.

Moya was the next person to emerge from the extended moment as she assured Mommie Dearest, 'He's gone, sweetie. It's okay. Everything is back to normal.'

At that point there was only one thing that I knew to be an absolute truth: nothing would ever be normal again, whatever 'normal' meant.

Mommie Dearest wailed at me, 'Why did you bring him here?! Why?' I hadn't seen her hatred boil over like that since the last time she tried to murder the man who was not our father.

For the first time in years I felt remorse for upsetting her, for hurting her. Now that I had finally succeeded it was less than bittersweet. The woman had been raped by her brother, our uncle, our father, and had obviously never recovered. She tricked Father Daddy into marrying her so that she wouldn't have to live with the shame. It was a terrible thing to do, but desperate times call for desperate measures. Moya eased our shaken mother toward the house and told me, 'I think you'd better go. I'll take care of her.'

Rattled, I shuffled into driver's seat and was about to start the engine when Mommie Dearest screamed at me again, only this time she sounded less wounded, more diffused, more like her self-medicated old self, yet she seemed inquisitive in a way that she never was, 'Why did you tell me he was dying?'

'I thought they were the same person.'

Mother broke away from Moya and raced over to the me, 'So my brother is the one who is dying? Why didn't you tell me?'

'Until this afternoon I had no idea you had a brother.'

Mother opened the passenger door and sat down, 'You must take me to him. Right now, Thompson!' Her eyes pleading while her mouth demanded, 'Please!' only not at all in the form of a question.

Seeing her outside the house was alarming enough, but trying to imagine her wandering around Manhattan in her threadbare bathrobe was downright terrifying. And yet, somehow I knew that Emily Post would make an exception to the proper dress code for that special moment when a mother first introduces her brother to their son.

'Do you want to change? I don't mind waiting.'

'There's no time, Thompson. Please just go.'

I had no idea why she wanted to see this monster but I felt compelled to protect her while she made peace with our father, her incestuous rapist brother, before he died.

WE WHIZZED through Westchester and Co-Op City in silent denial while the thick New York air swirled around the convertible. As we approached the Tri-borough

Bridge, the city's newly formed skyline continued to grow in stature as if it were filmed using time-lapse photography. I accidentally drove through an EZ-Pass lane before realizing that EZ-Pass didn't exist back in 1983 when Mother had chained the Porsche to the chestnut tree. I ended up causing quite the rush hour back up, ultimately receiving a lecture from an annoyed toll booth collector with the promise of receiving a summons by mail.

The FDR Drive was crawling, as were my nerves. Somewhere south of the Queensboro Bridge was when rush hour traffic ground to a halt beneath the tall buildings which straddled the highway. The urban camouflage gave me the courage to pull out the pipe. I ducked out of sight from the surrounding drivers so I could take a quick hit but Mother immediately flipped out. I knew she would but I didn't care. I had nothing else to hide.

'Please tell me that's not a crack pipe?'

'No.'

'No you won't tell me, or no you're not smoking crack? Please be more specific.'

'No to both. It's a crystal meth pipe.'

'Well that certainly puts me at ease,' she quipped before she looked back to the road and screamed, 'Thompson!' and when I looked up from the pipe I noticed a shady man in a trench coat disappear beneath the hood as soon as I slammed on the brakes and narrowly avoided a rear-end collision with the yellow cab in front of us.

I panicked, 'Did I hit him?'

'Hit the car? I don't think so.'

'The man!'

'What man?'

I jumped out and rushed to the front of the car as the angry commuters behind me started to lay on the horn. I got down on my knees to look underneath the car but there was nobody. No body.

'We're good,' I lied, calmly climbing back into the Porsche, desperately glancing in all the non-missing mirrors to locate the now-missing Feds. I tried to be nonchalant, scanning the stop-and-go traffic for federal agents as my hand patted around the floor mats, trying desperately to locate the very same Bic lighter you had virulently claimed I stole from you before the last taping. Which in retrospect turned out to be the very last taping.

'You're going to get us both killed!'

I said, 'You say that like we're both actually living.'

Mother began to rattle on about how I was much too high to drive, only she seemed more concerned than judgmental. Unfortunately she was right, but we were both much too fucked up to give a shit. I reluctantly put the pipe away, but that was mostly because I was paranoid about the unmarked, late model sedan in my rearview mirror that was obviously harboring the missing Fed, even if he was just another one of those terrifying figments.

That's when Mother found the stack of letters from Aunt Pudge and asked, 'What are these?'

'Those are letters from your sister, Pudge.'

'Why do you have them?'

'She asked me to give them to you.'

'You met her?' Then her tone turned desperate, 'Does she know?'

'No. But he abused her, too. You should visit with her. I think she'd really like that.'

Mother stopped asking questions after that and we both let the silence fill the void. She stared despondently out the window, looking at the world she had abandoned years ago. It was obvious that too much was happening at once for her so she placed the letters safely back on the floor mat without opening them. She proceeded to check out and drift away to her quiet place where she had spent the bulk of our childhood.

ALTHOUGH TRAFFIC eased, the unmarked car continued to follow me. No matter what lane I switched into, or what speed I drove, that late model, bright yellow Chevy had been tailing me since we crossed the Triborough bridge. A less discerning eye might mistake it for a taxi, but I knew better. Both Mother and Lady TomTom scolded me when I veered abruptly across three packed lanes of the FDR Drive so I could exit at 23rd Street at the last possible second without being followed.

Lady TomTom readjusted her route as we sped past the repetitive brick monoliths that comprised the northern border of Stuytown. After making what may or may not have been an illegal left onto Fifth Avenue at the Flatiron building, traffic moved swiftly until we approached a giant police barricade on 14th Street. I began to panic. I immediately looked into the sky and, as I suspected, the black helicopter was back, slightly in front of me, hovering above the urban canyon made up of luxury co-ops that lined Fifth Avenue. Until that point I had only been aware of being followed, but now they seemed to be anticipating where I was headed. The roadblock was intended to trap me, or rather you, because they obviously thought I was you. What the hell had you done to warrant this kind of police activity? The Feds wanted you so badly that they were willing to shut down one of Manhattan's major arteries and chalk it up to the terrorist attacks. And when I really thought about it, the whole World Trade Center mysteriously collapsing began to seem more and more like an elaborate conspiracy to lure us out of Hollywood so they could capture you.

The cops behind the barricades were diverting southbound traffic to turn east or west onto 14th Street but the idea of veering off course became overwhelming. Mother asked me, 'Is everything okay?' but by the time we reached the barricade everything was far from okay. A police officer motioned me to pull over and from the angry look on his face I wouldn't have been surprised if he thought I had been the mastermind behind the World Trade Center attack.

I didn't know what to do, so I froze. I needed to think. I began to wonder what you would have done had you found yourself in the same situation. The cop was motioning me to the left, Mother was yelling at me to turn right and Lady TomTom was urging me to continue straight ahead, taunting me by the fact that my destination was only a quarter mile away.

The cop screamed something unintelligible as he approached the car on foot, shaking his head, annoyed by my paralyzing ambivalence. It was definitely a frustrating Calgon moment and I desperately needed to be taken away,[43] just not by the Feds. Obviously someone had tipped off the cops, most likely Father Daddy, and I briefly thought about shifting into reverse so I could back out of the dire situation. Unfortunately there was a city bus so far up my tailpipe that it felt like date-rape.

I PLAYED DUMB and pretended that the cop was waving me down because I was famous. It seemed plausible at the time so I flashed him a big, dimpled smile and waved back to him as if I were on top of a float in the Macy's Thanksgiving Day parade. My plan definitely took him off-guard, if only momentarily, as he moved away from the barricade and began to walk toward us in a huff, to scold me, possibly arrest me. When he reached the

---

[43] HARRIED HOUSEWIFE: "The traffic. The boss. The baby. The dog. That does it. Calgon, take me away!" ANNOUNCER: "Lose your cares in the luxury of a Calgon bath. Calgon softens the water to leave skin feeling silky smooth. As it lifts your spirits. The soft, luxurious, frequent world of Calgon. Pamper yourself with a Calgon bath. Lose yourself in luxury."

driver's side and was no longer standing in front of the car, I pounded the gas pedal and popped the clutch. Mother braced herself as the Porsche crashed through the wooden blue barricades that read 'Police Line Do Not Cross.' It was very dramatic, very *Dukes of Hazzard*.[44]

Mother screamed and ducked her head deep into her lap as if she had been instructed by a flight attendant on how to prepare for a crash landing. There were lots of sirens, yelling, honking and possibly even a gunshot in my wake, probably because one or more of the cops were aiming at us, shooting at us. I screamed with rollercoaster-like abandon, racing down the last few barren blocks of Fifth Avenue, getting closer to the end of my quest for the truth. Or possibly just closer to the end.

I whizzed past The New School and peered into the rearview mirror even though I knew it was a bad idea. I hoped to find a bunch of lazy cops who were shrugging off my erratic behavior as the wild and crazy antics of another wacky celebrity. Unfortunately, there were no shrugs reflected in the mirror, just lots and lots of flashing red lights, pressed blue uniforms, gleaming white patrol cars, chasing me, aiming lots and lots of guns. All pointed at me.

I plowed past the upscale apartment buildings that lined Fifth Avenue. Pedestrians ducked for cover, some shrieked as if they were auditioning for the Janet Leigh part in *Psycho,* probably because of the gunshot which had punctured the front tire and rendered the power steering useless. Everything after that shot played out like a movie in slow motion. So slow, in fact, that even though I was

---

[44] *The Dukes of Hazzard* is an American television series that aired on CBS television network from 1979 to 1985. The show follows the adventures of cousins Bo and Luke Duke who live in a rural part of the fictional Hazzard County and race around in their customized 1969 Dodge Charger stock car, christened The General Lee. The show favored regular car chases, jumps and stunts in lieu of dialog and plot.

careening through the red light at the 9th Street intersection it felt like there was plenty of time to go get a tub of popcorn at the concession stand.

Sooner or later I barreled into a white Lexus parked on the street as Lady TomTom informed me, emphatically, 'You have reached your destination!'

MY FIRST INSTINCT should have been to swallow what little was left of the meth and jump out of the car, but instead I froze. I sat there in front of The Brevoort as a black raven flew down from the blue sky and perched itself on the top of the convertible's windshield. This one, however, was not at all threatening. It cocked its head back and forth, stared at me, one eye at a time, sizing me up before it burst into flames. Like a phoenix.

Moments later the police yanked me out of the car and tackled me to the ground. I was sprawled on the street, spread eagle while a cop was grinding my cheek into the pavement as I watched the black-eyed doorman, Petey the Pit Bull, emerge from the lobby, obviously to check up on the commotion. He recognized me and began ratting me out to one of the numerous cops and mysterious trench-coat men who had swarmed the area. Everyone pointed and whispered.

One officer patted me down and handcuffed my wrists so tightly that my fingers went numb. Another informed me of my right to remain silent. Since I was unable to move, someone yanked me into a standing position in such a way that practically ripped my shoulder out of its socket.

After that I was pushed toward Mother who was also cuffed and crying. We both stood in front of the old Porsche, which was pretty mangled but not totaled. Mother stared at the open hood, which had obviously busted open when I careened into the Cadillac. Instead of housing the turbocharged engine, the Porsche's trunk-space lived beneath its hood, and after the impact its contents had spewed out onto the street. The area was swarming with bomb-sniffing dogs, most of which seemed baffled by the few things which hadn't ripped open during the impact. Mother was being interrogated about the stuff and kept repeating, 'They're just old presents. For my son.'

I was struck by the fact that she specifically said 'son' singular, not 'sons' plural. Or 'twins.' I began to scan the toy-ridden crime scene with oodles of colorfully wrapped birthday and Christmas presents splattered along The Brevoort's sidewalk like Toys 'R Us road kill. A lifetime's worth. Make that a childhood's worth. Colorful *LiteBrite* pegs were sprinkled amongst *Parker Brother's Sorry!* cards. A pair of tweezers and lots of plastic bones from *Operation* were splattered around the asphalt like a war zone. The Evil Kenivel doll had only broken an arm, whereas several of the *Star Wars* action figures were missing limbs or had been completely decapitated. Michael Jackson's bestselling *Thriller* gave new meaning to shattering records, and the Weeble Wobbles had all fallen down. Every vertebrae of the Nintendo had been completely crushed, though the *Super Mario Brothers* and *Donkey Kong* cartridges somehow seem to have survived the carnage. A vintage Sony Walkman was in desperate need of media since the GoGo's and Culture Club cassettes were sprawled out amongst Milton Bradley's colorful, battery-operated *Simon* and eight giant D-cell batteries.

If something unpleasant happens to Santa Claus and there are no toys under the tree, was it really Christmas?

The taxi-turnabout in front of the Manhattan Co-Op had become a veritable tag sale on the *Island of Misfit Toys.*[45]

---

[45] In the classic Christmas television special, *Rudolph the Red-Nosed Reindeer,*

Toys I would have begged Santa to bring had Mother ever taken us to sit on his lap; toys we never got because Mother never went shopping because Mother never left the house.

Although the cops were confused by the sheer volume of collectible toys that were probably worth a small fortune on eBay, I was confused by the fact that there was only one of everything. If there's one thing that every parent knows about giving twins a gift, is that you must buy two of everything. The other thing that puzzled me on a quick examination of the To/From labels were that all of the presents were 'To: Me' and 'From: Daddy.' Which Daddy they were from I had no idea, but I hoped it was Father Daddy and not Uncle Daddy.

One cop was screaming at me, demanding to know if there were any bombs or explosives in the car. I shrugged and said, 'There might be a chemistry set?' even though I'm pretty sure there wasn't, mostly because I never wanted one of those. Another un-amused cop pulled a stack of envelopes from the glove compartment, which I initially assumed was the same one Aunt Pudge had given me, until he held it up and I realized that this particular stack of old letters was addressed to me. I was mesmerized by the cards, some of which were so old they had been mailed with ancient twenty cent stamps that needed to be licked. However the cost of postage was not what surprised me— it was the sender's name, a name as recognizable as my own, mostly because it was my own: Thom Thompson, Jr.

It hit me suddenly, while one, possibly all of the cops were simultaneously screaming at me, pushing me away from my presents, away from The Brevoort, away from

---

after Rudolph escapes the Abominable Snowman on a handy iceberg, he discovers the Island of Misfit Toys where unwanted playthings with cosmetic or physical flaws go to live with the island's ruler, King Moonracer, a brown winged lion, until he can find homes for them. What? Too esoteric?

Uncle Daddy's apartment. I began to fear that I would never get the chance to meet our Uncle Daddy before he went to hell, that I would not be able to reject the dying man's last wish to reconnect with me, that I would not be able to spit in his disgusting face.

I began to weep as the cop protected my head but hurt my neck as he shoved me into my blue vinyl, backseat prison.

I REMEMBERED WHEN we were about five, seven at most, and you came home for Christmas between switching boarding schools. We had to wake up Mommie on Christmas morning since she had overslept. For some unknown reason we were particularly excited that Christmas and I remember Mommie peeling her eye mask up to reveal a bloodshot eye. I whispered, 'Merry Christmas, Mommie,' as quietly as I could muster even though it was at least noon. Mother stared at us for an unbearably long time before she said, 'How much longer am I going to have to suffer through you believing in all this absurd Santa Claus business?'

I think that was the last Christmas we ever spent together. After Mother sent you off to military school, you stopped visiting us altogether. On Christmas break you would tag along with random roommates and call me to brag about the elaborate gifts that their families showered upon you. You were always trying to make me jealous. I remember one Christmas when I was a junior at Greenwich High, I just hid in the garage loft like a homeless person doing mounds of cocaine to usher in the holiday. Talk about a white Christmas.

2

NEW YORK'S FINEST interrogated me for what felt like days. I assured them repeatedly that I wasn't working for anybody. That I was not working for the terrorists, even though Julie Chen had definitely approached me weeks before to head up a covert operation with the code-name *Big Brother: Kabul*. That I was an actor from LA, not a very good one at that, not to mention a newly unemployed one thanks to a twin brother who dabbled in gay porn who had a penchant for impersonating me.

They played Good Cop/Bad Cop and filmed everything I said. The Good Cop begged me to eat something or take a sip of water, but my senses were heightened and the smell of the Bad Cop's poisoned offerings burned through my already scabby nostrils.

It was all very disconcerting until I finally invoked my Miranda Rights and demanded a lawyer. They, of course, immediately locked me up in what I assumed to be solitary confinement, obviously to keep a better eye on me, even though they all lied about how they were worried about my safety amongst the other prisoners. Or was it the prisoners' safety?

I STARTED COMING DOWN after that and everything became such a boring blur that it's hard to remember specific details. I remember being held next to another private cell that housed an irritating FBI informant disguised as a post-op homeless Tranny. She had this irritating habit of punctuating everything that came out of her mouth with a loud, 'Ha!' as if she had turrets. She asked me an endless array of probing questions and screamed endlessly, 'I will sue the NYPD for police brutality if I don't get my 'effing hormones. *Ha!*' Meanwhile, I felt like I had my own case of police brutality brewing thanks to the stench emanating from the Homeless Tranny's hormone-less vagina. Her last bath was obviously pre-op.

'Toto, I don't think we's in Kansas anymo'. *Ha!*'

I didn't bother looking up at her from my wafer-thin mattress as I said, 'Fuck Kansas.'

'Been there, 'effed that. If ya know what I'm sayin', Toto! *Ha!*' The fact that a tranny wouldn't use the F-word did nothing but confirm my theory that they had planted her there to spy on me. And later, after one of my tantrums—specifically the one where I pretended to be dead until a he entered my cell to check on me and I threw my tray of so-called scrambled eggs at him, screaming at the top of my lungs about how my human rights were being violated since they wouldn't give me a fucking Xanax. After that episode the Homeless Tranny began to lecture me, 'You know, nobody likes a potty mouth. *Ha!*'

I'M NOT SURE exactly how long I was incarcerated. It could have been days, possibly hours, maybe even weeks. The crash after my extended binge was really bad that time and eventually I realized it was in my best interest to shut the fuck up and pretend like everything was copacetic even though I was falling apart inside. It became increasingly emotionally taxing to ignore the Homeless Tranny in the midst of an early onset menopause, obviously brought on by her rapidly depleting estrogen levels. Being in jail felt like being on *Big Brother*, only with less irritating, yet equally fucked up individuals, all desperate for copious amounts of attention.

I prayed for Xanax since I was coming down hard, splayed out on a cramped, ¾-sized twin mattress, drowning in my own serotonin-deprived depression. I did nothing but obsess, uncomfortably, uncontrollably, about the paranoid decision I had made when they booked me. At that time, in lieu of contacting a lawyer, I decided that it was best to use my one and only phone call on Uncle Daddy. I became obsessed with seeing him before he went to hell.

EVENTUALLY A COP walked over to my cell, thankfully not the one I'd attacked with the plate of poisoned eggs. This particular cop looked like a fat Brian Setzer from the Stray Cats, only he was gasping for air between belching gulps from a freshly opened two-liter bottle of Sprite. He stood in front of the bars, pretending to read an article from *The Post,* although he had folded it in such an obvious way that I would get a nice, big, unobstructed view of my less-than-becoming mug shot on *Page Six* (which was surprisingly on page eleven or something equally pretentious).

Officer Seltzer belched more Sprite before he said, 'You look much taller in person, Princess.'

'Glass houses, big boy. Glass houses. *Ha!*' As usual the Homeless Tranny assumed that Officer Seltzer was talking about her, mostly because the Homeless Tranny assumed everybody was always talking about her. Obviously there's a fine line between narcissism and schizophrenia. Then she said, 'At least when I sit my ass down on the toilet it don't yell back, 'Get offa me!' That's right. I said it fatty. *Ha!*'

Officer Seltzer quipped back, 'The idea of you sitting on a toilet is not something I ever wanna imagine. Besides I was talking about the other princess. The famous one. Or should I say infamous?'

The Homeless Tranny ran over and grabbed *The Post* through the steel bars. She read like a fourth grader with dyslexia, moving her lips slowly before settling on pronunciation, adding extra syllables to monosyllabic words like 'porn' and 'meth.'

Officer Seltzer said, 'Today's your lucky day,' and then proceeded to leave me dangling, impatiently waiting for his cliff hanger to resolve as he gulped another liter of Sprite.

The Homeless Tranny asked, 'Whose lucky day?' as if she'd ever had a lucky day in her life.

'Someone posted your bail.'

My insides began to pound as if I were at a really loud club, the bass thumping through my heart, 'Who?' I begged. 'Is it my father?'

The Homeless Tranny said, 'Lucky you. My father wouldn't never spend a dime on bail for his only daughter.'

'Hate to break it to you, sweetheart,' Officer Seltzer said as he unlocked the cell door for me, 'but this is the men's ward and you ain't nobody's daughter.'

He unlocked my cell as the Homeless Tranny made vindictive sucking noises through her rotting, lipstick-stained teeth while readjusting whatever she was hiding between her legs.

SOME MACK TRUCK-SIZED, monotone lady cop slowly read the conditions of my release and made me sign statements that I was being released with the understanding that I must return to the state of California on my own recognizance and enter a state recognized drug rehab facility, yadda-yadda-yadda. I signed my way through the red tape until she returned my personal belongings (minus my stash and paraphernalia) in a sterile Ziploc bag that thankfully included the stack of Aunt Pudge's letters. I narcissistically scanned the precinct for an unfamiliar face that looked like an older version of me. Of us.

My eyes skipped over all the uniformed police officers, the easily identifiable plain-clothed detectives, any person of color, all the women and any man under forty. I literally stopped in my tracks when I locked eyes with the one person that did not fit any of the categories of my desired demographic.

I WAS EQUALLY stunned as I was undeniably deflated to find Mother standing in the middle of the Police station. It was the second time she'd been out of the house in decades, but at least now she was dressed. She was wearing pearls and a fashion-less Ann Taylory-Brooks Brother-ish outfit that somehow hadn't been destroyed by moths even though it had been hibernating in her closet since the early eighties. Mother stood out like a thumb so sore that it had most likely been fractured. I had no idea what to say, probably because it's the first time in years that I'd seen her sober (or close enough), while I was simultaneously sober. Neither of us knew what to do or how to behave in such an extraordinary, twelve-steppy circumstance.

Habitually, I scanned the waiting room for a drug dealer. Although several thugs fit the profile, I realized they were probably undercover cops. Young Johnny Depps from *21 Jump Street*[46] (but much less good-looking). The tension

---

[46] *21 Jump Street* is an American television series focused on a squad of youthful-looking undercover police officers investigating crimes in high

mounted as Mommie threw the handle of her handbag beneath the crook of her arm and made her shaky, yet stately way across the room, toward me. Slowly. Calculated. Rehearsed. It was the first time in years I'd seen her out of her threadbare robe. I was completely frozen as the chill of her icy lips barely braised my cheek in the form of a kiss before she said, 'It's hard to believe, but you actually look better than you did the other day. Prison becomes you.'

'Why are you here?' I asked, deflated even though I knew the odds of Uncle Daddy showing up, let alone still being alive, had been slim to none.

'You're welcome,' she snapped back.

We drew a lot of attention from random strangers, partly because two WASP's from Greenwich and their black, uniformed maid tend to stand out amongst the typical denizens of a New York City police precinct. But when it became readily apparent that one of us also happened to be half-assed famous, random derelicts began to press in as if we were at a premiere, on the red carpet, standing next to a wildly rotating, massive-wattage Klieg light.

Obviously well aware of our constraints, Mother gestured toward a small flock of cameramen and Stalkerazzi waiting to crucify me and said politely, 'You have a few friends waiting for you outside.'

I FOLLOWED THEM through the glass doors of the precinct, directly into the eye of the media storm. Strobe-like photo flashes began to strike away at us like heat lightning. Unintelligible questions swirled around dangerously like patio debris in a category five hurricane.

---

schools, colleges, and other teenage venues. Johnny Depp starred as one of the cuter Narcs.

I asked a bit too loudly, unnerved, 'Where did you park?' Mother pointed in the direction with her panicked eyes since her unkempt cuticles were busy digging deep into the skin of my forearm. People terrified her even more than they terrified me when I was sober.

I dragged Mother through the growing mob of paparazzi and passersby, feeling like a lifeguard, desperately trying to keep her from drowning within the first crowd she'd been subjected to in twenty years. Staying afloat in order to avoid a murky death by tabloid headlines proved to be difficult. So-called reporters screamed nasty things, desperately trying to offend me into doing something offensive for their cameras to document. Luckily I was sober enough to hold both my breath as well as my tongue as I navigated through the tabloid tsunami that was attempting to drown us in the murky depths of the extremely shallow situation.

'For some reason the police department has closed the whole block to car traffic so we had to park around the corner,' Mother informed me, even though I was highly aware of the situation due to the lack of yellow cabs available to hail.

We swam slowly through the school of slimy paparazzi fish, treading water as we worked our way toward the Avenue. Miraculously, I found a mysterious hole in the throng of people, just big enough for the three of us to squeeze through and escape. It was as if we were in a three-legged race, dodging red-eye reduction flashes from digital SLRs as they screamed obscenities and attempted to get a rise out of me.

Whoever said, 'Hey Meth Mouth! Show us your pearly whites!' also stuck his foot out and tripped me. I lost my balance and ended up stumbling into a makeshift sidewalk memorial made up of candles, flowers and school children's drawings. I accidentally knocked over one of the candles and wax splattered over a souvenir-sized, plastic model of the Twin Towers.

Mother yanked me back to my feet and pulled me from the paparazzi, leading me toward safety. Our power dynamic had somehow shifted and she'd assumed responsibility of our getaway, like a real mother would instinctively protect her child from danger, which, until now, had never been instinctive for her. As Mother continued to pull me further from harm's way, I began to realize that, perhaps for the first time since The Accident, I was actually trusting her.

I FELT SAFER as we rounded the corner even though a crowd began to gather behind the Porsche, the damaged hood had been jerry-rigged shut with a makeshift bungee cord. Honestly, seeing the bashed up car on the road surprised me even more than the fact that Mother had willingly left the house, again. I asked, 'You drove the Porsche?' as I swatted away microphones while being bombarded with inane questions from overly made-up TV reporters.

'Someone had to get it out of impound. Now hurry up. Your father has gone to great lengths to meet us for lunch and he doesn't have much time before his wife gets back.

And with that everything began to make sense. Mommie Dearest's first field trip outside the house in twenty years, her vintage outfit, her newfound, untapped tenacity. Her ulterior motive became undeniable.

A chorus of 'Over here, Thom! Look this way!' filled the expanding void between us, but their presence faded as equally as my focus heightened.

She pulled me toward the restaurant as the words slipped out of my mouth, 'You're not disgusted by him?'

Her response was immediate, as equally passionate as it was upsetting, 'Of course not. He's my brother.'

The media continued to buzz around us, parasitically making a wise bet on a dramatic crescendo to the tabloid induced frenzy. Mommie Dearest nervously fixed her perfect bun for the camera as she began to plead, 'Your father is very ill and he's gone to great lengths to arrange a private meeting with you. I know you crave this kind of attention but we really must go.' Her eyes begged me to follow her but, as I learned from Reality TV, the show must go on.

If something happens off camera on a Reality TV show, is it real?

After that there was a long, dramatic Jerry Springer-ish beat where I could almost hear the whirring of the camcorders. The whirring, however, ended up being a low-flying fighter jet which we all watched apprehensively, almost like a collective Chicken Little waiting in dread for the sky to fall. Again.

'Have you ever wondered why I crave this kind of attention?' I gestured toward the camera lenses, focused tightly their one-manned celebrity safari as they collectively zoomed in for the kill. 'Maybe it's because it's the only attention I ever got.'

'Well you can have it all to yourself because I've had enough of this circus. Your father is dying and I won't keep him waiting.' Then she turned toward the restaurant, but stopped in her tracks when she noticed a determined woman pushing a frail man's wheelchair through the crowd, toward us. Mother's face turned pale as the woman grabbed her arm in an overly familiar, yet practically crazed way. Although she held our mother captive, the stranger kept looking at me, like a psychotic fan who was one creepy threat away from receiving a restraining order.

THE STRANGER'S PALM sliced through the air and slapped Mommie Dearest's face so hard that you could've dusted her cheek for fingerprints. The paparazzi egged them on with their flashes, but the impending battle never came to fruition because Mother seemed to welcome the slap. She practically offered her other cheek as if she were Jesus.

The stranger screamed, 'You are a sick, *sick* woman!'

Mommie Dearest focused only on the disabled man breathing oxygen through a tube, but he kept his eyes on me. Mommie Dearest dropped to her knees and said, 'I just wanted him to meet his son.'

They all looked at me with pity as the stranger pushed Mother aside and attempted to inch Uncle Daddy's wheelchair through the crowd. The man gave me a pathetic, puppy-dog look, begging me for attention, but I looked away because I did not want to remember this man who was not our father, this man who ruined us instead of raising us, this selfish man who wanted me to forgive him. Instead of forgiving, I chose to forget.

Mommie Dearest begged Uncle Daddy's wife to reconsider as she grabbed her shoulder and put words to my biggest fear, 'We were in love.'

But Uncle Daddy's wife wasn't buying it, 'You were brother and sister!'

Mommie Dearest grabbed onto my arm as if I hadn't already heard her confession, 'We were in love.' My body reflexively pulled away as the last thing I wanted to do was touch her.

Eventually Mommie Dearest eased herself into the Porsche and ground the gears into reverse as the car jerked backward and almost plowed through the ever-expanding crowd of ambulance chasing reporters and rubberneckers as if she were Lizzie Grubman.[47]

I STOOD ON THE STREET, alone, surrounded, overwhelmed, sober. My first instinct was to call you, but that was more about needing to score than share my sob story with you. Some things were better left unsaid. Regardless, my ulterior motives didn't matter much since you never picked up.

My second instinct was to hail a cab, to escape, to disappear, but when the cabbie asked me, 'Where to?' I had no idea how to answer.

For a while we drove around aimlessly with the meter running. We made a lovely loop around Central Park before heading down the West Side Highway along the Hudson, toward the thickening stench of burning plastic which did nothing but get me jones-ing for some hot rails. The cabbie drove as far south as he could until the police had the road blocked off for emergency vehicles, yet not as a trap for me as my paranoia had assumed the last time I tried to go south of 14th Street. We waited for the traffic cop to wave us away while this expansive, overly peppy roar emanated from the sidewalk. When I asked what was happening, the Middle Eastern cabbie with a consonant-free name pointed out proudly, 'They're cheering on the emergency workers.'

Cool air conditioning escaped as I rolled down the window and craned my neck to further investigate. Thousands of New Yorkers were mysteriously lining both sides of the empty highway as if they were watching a parade. They cheered, clapped and waved handmade signs for Firemen dangling from their big red rig as if they were

---

[47] Lizzie Grubman is well known as a publicist for celebrities such as Britney Spears, Jay-Z and the Backstreet Boys. On July 7, 2001, after being asked by security guards to remove her Mercedes from a fire lane, Grubman drove her SUV into a crowd of people in the Hamptons, injuring 16 people. Grubman was alleged to have made an inflammatory statement before striking her victims with her vehicle: "F*** you, white trash." Assuming the *** stands for UCK, Lizzie Grubman doesn't sound like the nicest gal.

dignitaries. The same applause was repeated for the police car that zoomed past us, and even the Con Ed truck behind them, all headed into the eye of the storm via the shoulder lane. I'd never seen anything like it. The crowd was peppered with wildly waving American flags and I was completely overwhelmed by the pervasive sense of abundant gratification and patriotism. People cheered in such a spirited, heartfelt way that my jaded heart had no choice but to believe them. The signs said things like, 'We ♥ U!' and 'We will never forget!' and a bunch simply said, 'Thank You!' It wasn't long before all those happy signs and happy people made me remember that if I ever wanted to feel happy again, then I needed to score.

I TOLD THE CABBIE to take me back to the W Hotel and received a warm welcome from the concierge (who, incidentally, no longer had the appearance of an FBI informant), 'Welcome back, Mr. Thompson.' I smiled, mostly because I was relieved that you obviously hadn't overstayed my welcome and burned down the hotel or received multiple complaints from multiple guests over disturbing shrieks emanating from the room during your eight-hour fisting session.

My knees swooned again as the elevator swept me up to the twentieth floor, but I thought I might actually faint when I entered the room and was immediately overwhelmed by the pungent combination of poppers, meth and sex. It was as if a sweaty marathon runner had tried to stop a plastic shower curtain from burning by dousing it with cat piss. Needless to say it smelled delicious.

I walked into the bedroom which was still overflowing with boys, some familiar, some new. The Twinky Asian and the Latino Bottom Feeder were amongst the regulars, but days of orgasm-less sex had taken its toll. Most of the dicks had been rubbed raw, purple actually, and the Twinky Asian was literally raising his rump toward me as if he were one of those skunks living in Mother's swimming pool. Perhaps he was attempting to spray me with the enormous load of cum that seeped from his contracting anus.

YOU WERE SITTING on the bed, naked, surrounded by strangers, barebacking one another. A leather belt was wrapped tightly around your withering bicep which you held onto, tightly, with your gnawing teeth. The Latino Bottom Feeder searched desperately for a vein that hadn't collapsed or gotten infected. 'I dunno, man. This arm is worse than the other one. Maybe you should give it a rest. Hit the pipe for a change.'

The fact that your arms were littered with track marks didn't seem to bother you as you ordered the Latino Bottom Feeder to 'Shoot downstream from the last shot.' You tightened then loosened your fist before pulling the belt a half notch tighter. You looked the other way, away from the needle, closing your eyes while he slammed your vein and brought you back to so-called life.

I was standing directly in front of you when you opened your eyes again. You had this slightly crazed look, probably because your good eye was ridiculously more dilated than your bloody one. I spoke loudly and clearly, enunciating each word like a speech therapist because I needed you to hear me. To fully understand me. 'I want you out of here. I don't care where you go, I don't care what you do, and I really don't care what the fuck happens to you. I want you out of my hotel room and out of my life.'

Your good eye stopped twitching when you looked at me and said, 'I can't leave you,' as if we were Siamese twins without the choice to separate.

I knew the only power I had over you was to cut you off like a cancerous tumor, so I walked over to the coffee table, picked up the rest of your stash, my stash, and shoved it into my pocket. Then I pulled you out of bed and grabbed some random clothes as I escorted your naked, withering body to the suite's door and pushed you outside. I threw random clothes into the hallway and attempted to slam the door closed but you weren't having it. You held the door open with your bare foot while you stared at me and said, 'I'm already gone.' Eventually I won the battle and pushed the door shut, separating us with a brief hydraulically controlled click of finality.

TIME BECAME A BLUR. Perhaps it may have stopped. I have no idea how long I was shacked up in that hotel room. It was definitely days, although it was hard to judge since the blackout shades were never opened. The only time I left the bedroom was to take the odd piss or scream at the maid through the peephole and tell her to leave us alone. I couldn't begin to count how many guys had fucked me. All I know is that each time someone re-posted the party on Craigslist, there was a constant stream of new dick. I begged them all to bareback me, to let me be their cum dump, to breed me as if I were Rod Hard, as if I were you. And I didn't stop begging until some guy who looked like Grizzly Adams pulled his fist out of my insatiable ass and it was covered in blood.

Nobody seemed too concerned; mostly they told me to give my ass a rest for a little bit and go have a hit on the pipe. At the time it seemed like pretty sound advice.

Since we had long since run out of toilet paper and towels, I shoved someone's filthy white sock between my ass cheeks to stop the bleeding. Then I waddled toward the living room on a quest to find the pipe. I don't know how I could've missed you in the corner, probably because I was too busy crushing the crystals on the coffee table, or maybe because the shades had been drawn and the only light came from the plasma TV playing lame hotel porn.

I don't know whose shit I was smoking, but it was good. Really pure. Too pure. I remember feeling so intensely good that I couldn't remember where I was? What time of day it was? Or what city for that matter? Like Daddy's convertible, I had ripped my top off and exposed myself. I had converted. Seroconverted.

I remember peeking out the curtains, probably to help remind me of my whereabouts. It was a beautiful day. Sunny and particularly clear. The World Trade Center was still gone, but the smoke pouring from Ground Zero was not. Although I felt ambivalent about my surroundings, I was undeniably still in New York. I fired up the lighter and took a hit from the puddle that formed in the bulbous part of the burnt glass pipe. I specifically remember inhaling, challenging myself to hold the smoke in my lungs as long as I could. But when my naked body turned its back on the unsettling skyline and I noticed you, I began to choke uncontrollably.

You were blue. Hanging from a noose in the corner that you had jerry-rigged from an air conditioning duct in the ceiling. The desk chair which you had been standing on had long since toppled beneath your dangling purple feet. You swayed back and forth, ever so slightly, like a wind chime, put into motion from the rush of Freon-chilled air pouring from the vent.

How long had you been hanging there? How had none of the tricks in the massive orgy ever noticed that their host was suffering from rigor mortis? I wanted to scream, needed to, but I was unable to emit anything beyond a hacking cough. It felt like I was having another one of those frequent nightmares where my voice wouldn't work. I ran into the hallway, naked, uncontrollably coughing for help. Ironically the terrified maid who found me assumed I was choking to death and attempted to do the Heimlich maneuver.

1

I WON'T BORE YOU with the details of
rehab since you already know that old song and dance, but
by the time the Betty Ford clinic approved my trip back to
New York for the funeral, commercial flight had become a
whole new bird. I was shocked when LAX literally
confiscated my nail clippers from my toiletries because
they were considered a security risk. I didn't argue. Nobody
did. Except for the White Trash couple dressed in
matching white sweat suits. They refused to board the
plane if the crew allowed the 'terrorist wearing the towel on
his head' to fly.

The red-eye was practically empty and uneventful except
for the two crying babies who were being ignored by their
mother since she was too busy sizing up suspicious
passengers. Mostly I passed the time flirting with the
Frosted Flight Attendant who winked at me before takeoff when he told me to stow my tray table.

Like most everything else that happened now, the wink
felt like a trigger. Even the hint of sex made me long for a
hit off the pipe. I found myself pulling my sleeves down to
cover what was left of my healing track marks and
counting out my second twenty-five days of sobriety on my
fingers while the Frosted Flight Attendant grilled me about
Big Brother. I'd only had one slip and it was right after
completing my twenty-eight days at Betty Ford. At the time
I felt fan-fucking-tastic, but when the binge ended I was
disgusted with myself because I really wanted to make it to
thirty and get that flimsy-ass A.A. coin.

If something unpleasant happens in rehab and there are no parents left to blame, did it really happen?

I didn't sleep a wink as I flipped continuously, endlessly through the same thirty-six channels of DirecTV while watching the sun rise out my window. We landed around six a.m. to zealous applause mostly because all the passengers were obviously thrilled by the fact that they were still alive, ironically the most jubilant applause came from the guy in the turban.

I told Aunt Pudge that I was fine with taking a taxi but she insisted that Father Daddy pick me up after my red-eye landed at JFK. It became obvious that they didn't trust me to be alone. The odd duo had apparently reunited and become bosom buddies during my lengthy stay at Betty Ford. Although they were a motley crew, together they were a force to be reckoned with.

It wasn't hard to find Father Daddy since JFK was like a ghost town, but for some unknown reason the man of cloth parked as far away from the terminal as was physically possible. I made fun of his ancient car as Father Daddy helped me put my luggage into his Chrysler LeBaron convertible, 'Talk about taking a vow of poverty.' Time had not been kind to the three-dimensional plastic wood that was literally peeling from the rusting side panels.

When it came to driving, Father Daddy had apparently also taken a vow of sluggishness, which shouldn't have been a problem since my flight had arrived extra early. I wanted to have plenty of time to get to Greenwich, enough to take a shower and change my clothes before the funeral, but for some unknown reason traffic had inexplicably ground to a halt as we approached the Whitestone Bridge.

Father Daddy said, 'Jesus H. Christ.'

I asked, 'What would Jesus say about your using his name in vain?' and then he gave me the finger, which really made me laugh. But what amused me most was that my sacrilegious, drug addicted ass had become inexplicably close to Father Daddy in a way that felt familiar, almost familial.

While the rest of Betty Ford's inmates were busy throwing emotional barbs and accusations of blame during 'Family Day,' ironically my non-father was the only one who bothered to visit me, which happened to be the same day Bush declared war on Afghanistan. Or was that the same day that neither rain, nor sleet, nor snow was able to stop the anthrax from being delivered all around the country? Even though the world was falling apart around us, Father Daddy still found the courage to get on a plane and fly across the country to pay his dues to his fake son. It was great to see him and he did his best to distract me from the plethora of my missing family members who had either recently died or currently in the process of killing themselves. It was funny how family issues could be more fierce than the relentless footage that played around-the-clock on the new hit series, *The War on Terror*, shot daily (pun intended) on location in Afghanistan. Who would've thought a war could have such a catchy theme song?

Finally Father Daddy spoke the obvious, 'We're not moving.' He turned on his FM-less radio to 1010 WINS and their tagline blared in Lo-Fi mono with less clarity than an important MTA subway announcement, 'You give us twenty-two minutes, we'll give you the world,'.

Unfortunately, the world that the 1010 WINS announcer was giving us left me a nostalgic for the good old days when Bill Clinton's cigar and Monica Lewinsky's cum-stained blouse were the only things that blemished the headlines.

Even the anchorman seemed sick and tired of delivering his atrocious news as he informed us that an American Airlines jetliner bound for Santo Domingo from JFK had plunged into a Rockaway neighborhood moments after takeoff. All three airports were shut down, as were all major bridges and tunnels serving the city, including the Whitestone Bridge, which was immediately apparent since we were boxed into unmoving bumper-to-bumper traffic. Unfortunately we had already passed the point of no return between the last exit and the closed toll booth.

'Are you okay?'

'Um, not particularly,' I said, surprised by the spontaneous tears that had begun to well up in my eyes. I cried all the time now. For any little thing. Every little thing. It had been a long time since I had felt anything real.

Father Daddy shut off the radio and assured me, 'Don't worry. We'll make it to the funeral on time. You'll be able to make your peace with him. For better or worse, he was your father.'

'My mother and father were brother and sister and had a consensual sexual relationship,' I reminded him. 'I'll never have peace.'

'Yes, you will. You'll see,' he stated this with a degree of priestly authority that made his lie rather comforting.

'Thanks again for coming to get me.' I wanted to change the subject. Needed to. I was working hard in therapy to actively appreciate people who were good for me, good for my recovery, rather than try to scare them away so I'd be able to justify their inevitable disappearance. My therapist told me I had to believe in my own happy ending. Not happily ever after, of course, but for the first time in my life I was willing to aim for happier.

THE NEXT THING I knew Father Daddy was shaking me awake with his hand on my knee. I blurted out, 'Hands off the Altar Boy!' but he had absolutely no sense of humor about the touchy issue (pun intended again) as he pulled off I-95 at Exit 3 in Greenwich.

He said, 'We probably missed the service so I think we should go straight to the cemetery.'

'How long was I asleep?' I wondered aloud with a gravelly voice.

'They closed the bridge for over two hours, but the news is reporting that it's just a tragic accident. Not another terrorist attack,' he said relieved, as if a terrorist-free plane falling from the sky was something to feel good about.

Father Daddy drove through backcountry Greenwich and pulled his old yellow jalopy into St. Mary's Cemetery. He parked the rust bucket alongside a road clogged with imported Mercedes, BMWs and Lexuses, most of which adhered to the traditional funeral dress code of shiny metallic black. I noticed Daddy's Porsche parked across from the hearse because it stuck out like a broken thumb, still in dire need of repair after my 'accident.' Mother was sitting shotgun, watching the funeral from the safety of her bucket seat, and Moya was cast in her new role of *Driving Miss Daisy*. I averted my eyes when Mommie Dearest waved at me.

The funeral had already begun, so Father Daddy and I walked conspicuously toward the small crowd surrounding Uncle Daddy's empty casket, hovering around the familiar grave site as they took turns throwing handfuls of dirt onto the empty casket. By the time I reached the group, I was already suffering from an extreme case of déjà vu. These people, these relative strangers, alleged relatives, did not seem particularly distraught over Daddy's death, or perhaps that was me projecting my ambivalence upon them.

Aunt Pudge didn't come, couldn't come. Surprisingly when I talked to her on the phone she seemed to be at peace with the fact that they were burying her nemesis in the family plot. She wasn't worried about spending eternity lying next to him since she wanted to be cremated. 'After all,' she told me, 'I'd never fit into a casket!'

Although I used to assume I knew everything there was to know after my twenty-one years on the planet, after twenty-eight days of sobriety the only thing I knew for sure of was that I knew nothing. Nothing made sense. I think the main reason I wanted to come to Uncle Daddy's funeral, wanted to come to our father's funeral *again*, was to make sure that it really happened this time.

I glanced around the Thompson family plot and took note of my long lost relatives who made up Uncle Daddy's eternal new neighbors. I realized that our paternal grandfather, Thompson Thompson, Sr., had died in the early nineties and I began to wonder if perhaps it was his funeral I remembered attending but confused it for Daddy's?

That's when a long lost memory began to flood into my head (which had become a common, yet disturbing occurrence those past few months in therapy). Although it meant nothing, I shivered as I remembered our Grandfather teaching us how to fill up his gargantuan Mercedes with gas using his own private gas pump that he had installed next to the four car garage on Raven's Nest Island.

I began to read the names etched into the gravestones of other dead Thompsons, but none seemed to ring a bell, most likely because they had all died long before we were born. But my heart dropped deep into my bowels when I recognized the name on one discreet little headstone, located directly next to Daddy's plot. *Your* name.

I was livid. Why on earth wouldn't they release me from rehab to attend my twin's funeral? Or at least mention it to me? The fact that I was detoxing was no excuse. However, it wasn't until I noticed the dates on the diminutive headstone that I literally began to weep. Timothy Thompson, Our Little Angel, September 10th, 1980 – October 7th, 1983.

If a tragic accident happens to a three year old who cannot bear to process it, does it really happen?

EVERYTHING CAME FLOODING back to me. Everything for which my shrink had been burrowing for months, deep within my subconscious. Everything I had long ago repressed. I remembered The Accident, vividly, the one that began Mother's depression as well as my denial. I remembered the funeral from long ago. You were the one who died when Mother drove us into the pool, not Daddy. It was your funeral I had attended all those years ago, not Daddy's.

Ancient pain burst from every cell in my body as if I were being electrocuted. The release felt excruciating, like an excavation, or actually more of an exhuming. Long lost memories began to reveal themselves, slowly, painfully, and were released in the form of shivers as my body began to convulse. I felt like Linda Blair in *The Exorcist.*[48]

I immediately ran away from the grave, your grave, away from the solemn group of related strangers. I ran as fast as I could because I felt like I was going to get sick. I didn't want to ruin Uncle Daddy's funeral, or ruin anything else anymore, so I covered my mouth and sprinted down the hill toward Father Daddy's old Chrysler as fast as I could.

Unfortunately the bile in my throat proved quicker than the soles of my shoes, and I ended up spewing an overly

---

[48] *The Exorcist* is a 1973 American horror film that deals with the demonic possession of a young girl named Regan and her mother's desperate attempts to win back her daughter through an exorcism conducted by two priests. There's lots of shaking beds and pea soup and a severely disturbing scene with a crucifix.

processed airline breakfast all over the dewy green grass. I ducked between a bush and a random car to hide my embarrassment as well as my overwhelming shame.

A warm hand began to stroke my back as the last bit of spittle drooled from my lips. I wiped my mouth and turned toward the soothing hand that belonged to Father Daddy.

I began to weep uncontrollably as I begged repeatedly for his forgiveness, 'I didn't mean to kill him.' He stroked the back of my head until eventually I began to hyperventilate. Mucus and tears poured from every orifice, but my messiness didn't seem to faze Father Daddy who accepted my soggy apology as naturally and unflinchingly as any parent would soothe their helpless baby.

'Shhh,' he whispered. 'It's okay.'

'It's my fault he died,' I hyperventilated. 'It was my fault.'

Father Daddy was unsure who I was talking about until I uttered your name. I recalled him swimming through the open sunroof to save us, yanking at your seatbelt, trying desperately to unbuckle you, but I made him stop. My seatbelt was already off so I grabbed him and clung around his neck, practically drowning him as my eyes plead with him to save me first. Before you. Instead of you. And he did.

After my admission it wasn't long before we switched roles and I had to comfort him as he began to beg for my forgiveness. It was difficult to decipher his apology, his confession amongst his tears, however he definitely assured me it was not my fault. For the first time it became clear why he had such an easy time amputating us from his life after The Accident.

AFTER FATHER DADDY learned the truth and exposed the incestuous relationship to her family, Mommie Dearest fell into a deep depression. Their marriage was over and Daddy was packing his clothes when he heard the massive splash as Mommie Dearest drove her Audi into the swimming pool. He ran outside and dove in the pool to save us but Mommie Dearest fought him off, scratching at his face to leave us be, to let us all drown.

All those years I had the story completely backwards. Mommie Dearest had not attempted to kill Daddy, she had attempted to kill us.

0

WHEN THE SMALL CROWD of mourners begin to disperse after Uncle Daddy's funeral ends, Father Daddy walks me over to your grave. He doesn't say much other than, 'It's all over.' I smile, knowing it has just begun. I ask him to give me a minute so I can pay my respects to my twin brother in private. I stare at your name while I try to take it all in. I feel like I'm at the bottom of an insurmountable mountain that I need to climb, at the edge of an endless ocean that I need to cross, at the beginning of a fruitless attempt to solve the equation of Pi. The idea of discerning what has truly happened from what I falsely remember seems absolutely daunting. Yet I am determined to untangle fact from fiction, to make sense of it, to learn from it.

I think about the incest. The intense shame I felt was not for the unspeakable act that we never committed in The Abbey's bathroom, it was for the unspeakable act that brought us into this world in the first place. The intense addiction I have is not for the pleasure that crystal meth gives me, it is for pleasurable escape it offers me from the truth. And the intense loss I have felt since The Accident was not for Daddy, it was for you. Nothing is what it seems. My emotional ambivalence is overwhelming and I decide to sort things out. Or, at the very least, attempt to.

I have no idea where to begin the story, but for some reason I am drawn to 9/11. It seems as good a place as any to start since it was the day my whole world changed. Which, ironically, has nothing to do with the fact that it was the day the whole world changed, too. Or possibly everything to do with it. So I sit down on the grassy area in front of your grave and begin to tell you my story. Our story."

9

"**EVERYBODY HATED ME.** The cast and crew. The hack director who had taken twelve hours to film a thirty minute sitcom. The writers and producers. The network suits. The studio audience who had mutinied and abandoned ship. My homophobic, latent homosexual stand-in who snuck peeks at me during wardrobe fittings. The paid laughers who were hired to sweeten the laugh track even though they had soured hours ago. Danny Pintauro who played the lady boy on *Who's The Boss?*[49] My overrated agent. My over-paid publicist. My overweight personal trainer. My boyfriend, Adam Roth. My executive producer, Adam Roth. The basket-case we referred to as Mommie Dearest.[50] Our dead father. Even you. My goddamn twin brother. *Especially you.*

EVERYBODY WAS HATING ME because everybody hated you, but as usual I'm getting ahead of myself. It was about T minus two hours before the taping when you appeared out of nowhere and burst into my trailer while I was memorizing last minute script changes.

---

[49] Danny Pintauro was the effeminate child-actor on *Who's the Boss?* who (spoiler alert) came out as gay in an interview with the National Enquirer tabloid in 1997.

[50] *Mommie Dearest* is a 1981 biographical drama film portraying Faye Dunaway as Joan Crawford, a driven actress and compulsively clean housekeeper who tries to control the lives of those around her as tightly as she controls herself. If the term, "No wire hangers!" means nothing to you, then perhaps you should put this book down now and sign up for a Netflix membership.

(continued on page 2)

ABOUT THE AUTHOR

Sean Meyrick Hanley was raised in Old Greenwich, Connecticut and is a graduate of Lewis & Clark College. He was on the writing staff of *The Nanny,* and recently co-created the sitcom, *Half-Share.* He currently lives in New York City and is in pre-production for a feature film called *Scamdance.*

The Convertible Life is his debut novel.

facebook.com/seanhanley
twitter.com/seanhanley7

Did you enjoy "THE CONVERTIBLE LIFE"?
Post your review at amzn.to/convertiblelife

www.ingramcontent.com/pod-product-compliance
Lightning Source LLC
Chambersburg PA
CBHW021032130626
46552CB00005B/1809